Traitor's Gold

Marshal Dave Stevens was a man on a mission: to capture the notorious outlaw and train robber Ned Bartell. A traitor to the Confederate cause during the Civil War, Bartell had caused the deaths of two thousand of his fellow soldiers and Stevens was not alone in wishing him to be brought to justice. There was Pinkerton operative Marie Devlin, whose dead brother Bartell had betrayed, and ex-army veteran Thorpe.

It was Bartell's greed for gold that wove the strands of fate to bring Stevens, Thorpe and the girl together – but would even their combined resolve be enough to ensure their survival against the vicious outlaws?

Traitor's Gold

Wade Dellman

ROBERT HALE · LONDON

First published in Great Britain 2006

ISBN-10: 0-7090-8073-5
ISBN-13: 978-0-7090-8073-2

Robert Hale Limited
Clerkenwell House
Clerkenwell Green
London EC1R 0HT

Typeset by Derek Doyle & Associates, Shaw Heath
Printed and bound in Great Britain by
Antony Rowe Limited, Wiltshire

CHAPTER I

MIDNIGHT CARGO

It was a little before midnight when Hal Fenton stepped out of his office at the railroad depot. The wind which swept along the deserted platform was bitterly cold and he cursed savagely under his breath at having to be on duty at this god-forsaken hour of the night. Two of the trains carrying large shipments of gold had been held up during the past three months, and now a different depot was chosen each time. It was his bad luck for Coulson to have been picked on this particular occasion with the temperature now well below zero and snow threatening from the north-east.

Carrying the red lantern in his right hand, he pulled his mackinaw jacket more tightly about his thin shoulders as he walked to the edge of the platform. Peering intently into the darkness, he strained to pick up the sound of the approaching locomotive above the shrieking of the wind.

The metal rails, just visible in the gloom, stretched away to the east as far as he could see. Then dimly, he made out the lights of the locomotive. The dismal wail of the whistle reached him a few moments later, carrying mournfully on the wind. Another two minutes and the wood-burner had pulled into the railroad depot, a plume of black smoke billowing from the funnel. He placed the lantern on the platform, clapped his hands around his thin chest and watched as the locomotive, connecting-rods clanking and steam hissing from the cylinders, drew slowly to a halt.

As Fenton grasped the lantern in numbed fingers, he picked out the sound of horses and wagons just outside the depot, followed by the harsh bark of orders.

One of the engineers stepped down from the cab and walked towards Fenton. 'They're on time for once,' he remarked. He had also heard the sound of the approaching detachment of troops.

Even as he spoke, the group of men came into view, a tall, efficient-looking sergeant in charge. There were fifteen altogether, several carrying large wooden boxes with rope handles. All had rifles slung over their shoulders.

The sergeant walked up to Fenton and held out a piece of paper. 'Sign this and we'll get them on board,' he said briskly. As Fenton scrawled his name at the bottom, the sergeant added: 'You've told no one about this?'

Fenton shook his head. 'I reckon I know better than that, Sergeant.'

'Good. The fewer people who know what's in those boxes, the better.'

'You think they'll still be safe from that damned outlaw?'

The sergeant gave what was supposed to be a smile. 'So you've heard these rumours too.'

'About Bartell? Sure, I've heard 'em and I'd say they're more than just rumours, Sergeant. That killer is somewhere in the territory between here and wherever you're goin' and that shipment o' gold is just the sort o' bait he'll go for.'

Sergeant Rutlidge carefully folded the piece of paper and thrust it into his tunic pocket. 'As far as I'm aware, there's no way he can know about it. I only received my orders this afternoon and apart from the two of us here, only one other man knows what's on this train, not even my men know what's in those boxes. As far as they're concerned, it's rifles and ammunition.'

There was a puzzled frown creasing the clerk's forehead as he said: 'One other man? Who might he be?'

'A federal marshal, name of Dave Stevens. Seems he's been after Bartell for some time. They reckon this gunslinger is wanted for several shootings along the border. Somehow, this marshal got the commandant's permission to travel with the train.'

'Well he ain't here. You sure he'll show up?'

'He's here already.'

Both men turned sharply at the sound of the voice. None of them had heard the tall man approach. Now he stood a couple of feet away, a faint smile on his lean features.

Fenton saw the hard eyes that drilled into him, noticed the twin Colts at the man's waist and the star on his shirt. He felt a little shiver pass through him. This was a man, he decided, he wouldn't want to tangle with.

To the sergeant, Stevens said evenly: 'I'll ride in the rear van if that's all right with you, Sergeant. If Bartell is fool enough to attack the train, we can get him and his gang from two sides.'

'Suit yourself, Marshal.' The sergeant gave a brief nod of acquiescence. 'I'm not expectin' any trouble but I appreciate an extra gun just in case.'

As Stevens made to move away, Fenton said tautly, 'Guess I ought to warn you. They reckon there's a bad storm brewin' somewhere to the west. It wouldn't surprise me if you run into a blizzard along the way.'

The engineer who had disembarked had approached and overheard. He grinned. 'Snow won't bother me none. That cowcatcher at the front will shift any that gets in our way. Reckon if there are any outlaws out there, they'll think twice about ridin' out in a snowstorm.'

'Then if he is foolhardy enough to try an attack, we'll be ready for him,' Rutlidge said harshly. 'My men have been given orders to shoot on sight.' To the engineer, he went on: 'You sure you've got sufficient fuel and water to take us the two hundred miles to Fort Amersham?'

'We've got as much as we can carry but it's possible we may have to make a stop along the line to take on more. If we do, it'll be at Felder Rapids.'

Sergeant Rutlidge considered that, then gave a brusque nod. 'Very well, I suppose that can't be helped. I want one of my men to travel with you on the locomotive. I'm takin' no chances this time.

He turned and began issuing commands to the waiting detachment.

Stacking their rifles against the depot wall, the men carried the gold-shipment to the waiting train, loading it into the van immediately behind the locomotive. Once this was done, they retrieved their weapons and made to climb on board.

Sharply, Rutlidge called: 'I want one of you men on the locomotive.'

The corporal stepped forward. 'I'll volunteer for that, Sergeant.'

'Very well, Cleaver. I want you to keep a sharp look-out at all times. Got that?' Nodding, the corporal followed the engineer while the other men pulled themselves into the van.

From beneath lowered brows Dave eyed each man in turn. He already had his suspicions that one of these men was in cahoots with Bartell, passing along vital information to the outlaw. Somehow, Bartell seemed to know exactly which train was carrying gold and which had been sent out as a decoy.

Twice before they had sent out empty trains, both guarded by a detachment of armed soldiers – and each time Bartell had failed to appear. From what he had been told, apart from himself, only the sergeant and the railroad clerk knew what was in those wooden boxes. The clerk he had already dismissed from his mind. He would have been told only a few hours earlier that the shipment would start from this particular depot.

Certainly that pointed to Sergeant Rutlidge being the informer but, somehow, he had a hunch that the other was innocent. For a moment he wondered whether to confide his suspicions to the sergeant, but then decided against such a move. If it were Rutlidge, the man would be instantly on his guard.

The engineer walked back to the locomotive and climbed into the cab, the corporal pulling himself up after him. A few flakes of snow were now drifting in the wind as Dave moved along the train and hauled himself into the rear van. He deliberately left the door partly open, seating himself with his shoulders against the side, out of the icy blast.

A moment later there came the forlorn sound of the whistle, a sudden hiss of steam, and they began to move. Shifting himself into as comfortable a position as possible, he checked the chambers of his Colts.

When he had asked the commandant for this assignment, he had expected his request to be turned down without any explanation. The Army was very reluctant to allow outsiders into their operations. He also knew they wanted Bartell almost as much as he did.

His first thought on learning this was that they wanted him only in connection with these robberies, but now he had the feeling there was something more; that it was to do with some incident that had happened during the recent war. Whatever it was, they seemed determined to bring him in, dead or alive.

*

Seventy-five miles west of Coulson there was a blizzard blowing up, straight off the high mountains to the north-east, when the five men rode up out of the night, oilskins draped over their shoulders, hats pulled down well over their eyes. The storm had begun barely half an hour earlier but already the snow was a couple of inches deep on the ground and the gleaming metal rails were only just visible.

Four of the riders sat low in their saddles, cursing the snow and wind which lashed mercilessly against their faces. The fifth, his mount hitched between the shafts of an army wagon, was a huge brute of a man, six and a half feet tall, his body broad, full-muscled, like that of a grizzly. His name, Ned Bartell, was to be found on a score of Wanted posters all along the frontier from the Mississippi to the far western border of Texas.

The law wanted him for more than a dozen killings, while the Army was keen to arrest him and try him for treason. Three years before, during the war between the North and South, he had made a good profit selling Confederate army secrets to the North. His activities had remained unsuspected by his superiors for almost two years. Then he had made his last, and biggest, mistake, passing along information concerning a surprise attack planned against the Yankee Army.

More than 2,000 troops had been slaughtered that night when they had advanced into a well-prepared trap. Suspicion had immediately fallen upon him.

Now his thick lips curled into a vicious grin as he recalled how easily he had succeeded in absconding before he could be apprehended, tried, and shot as a traitor. He knew there were still men who would never give up searching for him but that had long since ceased to bother him. Even though his name was now well-known along the Southern states, he was able to cover his tracks well. Now, with these four men working for him, and an informer passing along the vital information, he had already pulled off two successful train robberies.

He got down from the wagon and walked forward a little way, bracing himself against the vicious wind. In the storm, it was almost impossible to make out details clearly. He had not counted on such a bad storm as this blowing up to hamper his plans.

His companions swung down stiffly from their mounts and joined him. All were of the same breed as himself: outlaws, men who lived and died by the gun.

Sam Woodrow detached himself from the others. He pointed to their left. There, the narrow bridge spanned the deep gorge. 'It's goin' to be hell gettin' that gunpowder in place before that train comes through, Ned.'

'All right, it's goin' to be hell,' Bartell snarled. 'But the sooner we get started, the sooner we finish. We've got to have that bridge down and we've less than half an hour to get these barrels in place.'

He knew the men were cursing him for bringing

them out here in the middle of this blizzard, but he also knew that the thought of all the gold which that train was carrying would make them forget their discomfort. Greed for gold was the most intense driving force these men had.

Like himself, Woodrow and Ben Halleran were deserters from the Confederate Army. He had joined up with them in a little town along the Mexican border while on the run from the authorities. Pablo and Meninguez were drifters from across the state line with Mexico. If they'd ever had any other names, he'd never known them, nor had he bothered to ask. As long as they carried out his orders to the letter, he was satisfied.

'Do we wait until the train is on the bridge before we blow it?' Halleran asked.

Bartell swung on him savagely. 'Don't be a goddamn fool, Ben. I don't want that train down there at the bottom o' the gorge. I want it here where we can get at that gold.'

Sam Woodrow walked cautiously to the rocky lip of the gorge, his cape flapping about his thin body. His face was almost completely hidden beneath the hood but still the blinding snow managed to get into his eyes. In front of him, the irregular sides of the chasm dropped almost perpendicularly for more than 300 feet.

Looking down through the whirling snow, it was just possible to make out the narrow thread of the river at the bottom, flecked with white where it raced over its stony bed. If a man fell down there, he was finished. If the fall didn't kill him, that raging torrent would smash every bone in his body as it flung him against those rocks.

The bridge itself was the usual trestle structure with two massive pillars embedded in the gorge and criss-crossing struts beneath the rails. It looked flimsy, scarcely strong enough to bear the weight of a locomotive and wagons. Through the sheeting snow, he cast a critical eye over it, searching for the best places to put the barrels of gunpowder.

Turning at last, he walked back to Bartell. 'It's goin' to be mighty dangerous climbin' down there in this storm,' he shouted. 'We'll have to lash those barrels to the supports just beneath the rails.'

Bartell's teeth showed in a wolfish grin. 'Once we get our hands on that gold, it'll be worth it.' He gestured towards the wagon. 'You, Meninguez and Pablo get the explosive in place near the top o' those three struts yonder. And make sure the fuses are long enough to give you time to get back under cover. Now hurry – we ain't got much time.'

Bartell had spent two days planning the robbery and he didn't intend that anything should go wrong. From the information he'd received, this was by far the biggest consignment ever carried by the railroad. He knew it would be well guarded by riflemen but he was prepared for that.

After much deliberation, he had chosen this particular place to attack the train. Not only was there the bridge which, once successfully destroyed, would bring that train to a halt, but some fifteen yards from the railroad, on either side, stood a long line of high rocks. With his men concealed behind them, they could cut down the soldiers without exposing themselves to any return fire.

As the three men made their way towards the wagon, he turned every little detail over in his mind. He knew there was still a number of things which could go wrong; things over which he had little, or no, control. With the blizzard increasing in intensity, there was a distinct chance that the train might be delayed somewhere along the line or, perhaps, cancelled altogether until the weather improved.

Somehow, he doubted that they would cancel the train. They would go along with the belief that no one in his right mind would ride out in the teeth of this storm, even for that gold. The barrels of gunpowder were waterproof but they would have to lay the lengths of fuse with extreme care, well above the snow. He didn't want them being extinguished before the explosive did its work.

Calling to the two Mexicans, he pulled the barrels of explosive from the wagon, handling them as if they weighed nothing at all, handing each carefully to the others. Waiting until they had heaved them across their shoulders, he supplied them with a coil of stout rope and a long length of fuse, indicating where they were to be placed.

Their feet sliding precariously in the snow, the men trudged towards the bridge. He gave the third barrel to Woodrow and pointed towards the furthest bridge support. Hefting the heavy barrel over one shoulder, Woodrow eased his way along the bridge, clutching at the side with one hand to steady himself against the gusting wind.

The savage blasts now struck him ferociously from every angle, making his progress slow and perilous. Inwardly, he doubted Bartell's belief that this plan would work. Certainly there was a sharp bend about half a mile to the east where the railroad passed through a steep-sided cutting and the engineers would be forced to slacken speed at that point.

But with visibility down to only a few yards, he reckoned it would be virtually impossible for the engineer to realize the bridge was down before he had time to apply the brakes. This gold was going to end up at the bottom of the gorge no matter what happened and all of this would have been for nothing.

Meninguez had already lowered himself over the side and was struggling to ease himself into a safe position under the rails. Pablo had reached the middle of the bridge and was attempting to lower himself over the side. Edging past them, Woodrow moved on for a further fifteen yards, then lowered the barrel to the edge of the track.

Balancing himself precariously, he slowly worked his way over the edge, cursing as his feet slipped on the icy surface of the timber. It was only with a tremendous effort that he forced himself not to look down into that 300-foot drop beneath him. He knew that once he did that he would be unable to move an inch for fear of falling.

Sucking in a deep breath that burned in his chest, he lowered his left foot until it was wedged between two slanting timbers. There was now little feeling in his fingers as he clawed at the top of the bridge. Eventually he managed to work his body into a relatively safe position. Tears threatened to blind him as he coiled the thick rope around the top of the pillar; then slowly eased the barrel down until it was securely in place.

By now, he was so cold that the blood seemed to have frozen in his veins. Leaning back as far as he dared, clinging on with one hand, he somehow managed to loop the rope around the barrel, twisting it tightly around the upright, fumbling awkwardly as he knotted it.

Very carefully, he removed the small bung. He took out his knife, cut a small length off the end of the fuse and inserted the end into the barrel, looping it around the upright to ensure it remained securely in place. For almost a minute, he hung there, struggling to force some feeling back into his frozen limbs. Then, gripping the edge of the bridge, he succeeded in swinging himself up.

For a moment he lay there, the bitter air congealing the sweat on his back and shoulders. Then, steadying himself, he got to his feet. Now that the worst, and most dangerous, part was over, he felt easier in his mind. Very slowly, he let out the fuse, running it over the low rails that ran along the side of the bridge.

Pablo and Meninguez had already loaded the other barrels into position and were waiting at the end as Bartell lumbered up. 'Everythin' ready?' he asked gruffly.

The three men nodded.

'Good. Then get the wagon and horses under cover, well away from here. I don't want any o' the mounts spooked by the blast.' Turning, he added, 'You stay with me, Sam.'

Once the others had gone, Bartell walked to the rim of the canyon, peering into the storm, running his gaze along the bridge. Already, the snow was forming into deep drifts of white across the rails. At last he was satisfied that the explosive had been placed where he wanted it.

Swinging on his heel, he said sharply: 'Give me five minutes and then light the fuses. We're still on schedule. That train will still be miles away. Nobody on board will see or hear the explosions. Whatever happens, I don't want to give 'em any warning o' this.'

Woodrow watched as the other's mountainous figure disappeared into the blizzard. Inwardly, he prayed that nothing would go wrong. More than once he had found himself on the wrong end of Bartell's violent temper, had seen him shoot down a man who had crossed him.

When he was certain all of his companions were under cover, he pushed his way through the piling drifts to where the three fuses hung from the nearest upright. Finding what little shelter there was from the howling wind and snow, he struck a sulphur match, shielding it with his body as he applied the flame to the ends of the fuses.

He waited for a few seconds to ensure they were all burning correctly and then ran along the rails, lurching from side to side, before swinging away towards the rocks. The others were all crouched down behind the massive boulders as he dropped down beside them. A full minute went by and the silence around them intensified.

Bartell uttered a savage oath. 'Goddamnit! Something's wrong. That explosive should've gone off by now.' He made to thrust himself to his feet.

Then the powder went off, the triple-explosions so close together they blended into a single roar, echoes bouncing from the canyon walls. A vast sheet of flame speared into the air above the gorge. Rock and thick pieces of timber showered down among the boulders.

Pushing his bulky body hard against the rock, Bartell waited until the last of the debris had fallen. Then he got to his feet. Slowly, his companions did likewise. Moving cautiously out of cover, he surveyed the results of their handiwork.

The entire centre of the bridge had collapsed into the canyon. Long lengths of metal rails had been twisted like putty. The snow-laden gale, whistling along the ravine, had hurled the remnants of the structure into the swiftly rushing river at the bottom.

'Excellent.' Bartell slapped his gloved hands together, his lips twisted into a satisfied grin. He swung on the others. 'Keep the horses out o' sight and take up your positions on both sides o' the track. Don't open fire until they open the doors. There's no sense in wastin' precious ammunition.'

'How many soldiers do you reckon they've got on

the train?' Woodrow asked.

'Fifteen or twenty. That's my guess.'

Woodrow whistled thinly through his teeth. 'That many?'

Bartell rubbed at the irritating snow and ice that had formed on his cheeks and beard. 'Hellfire! You don't expect the Army to send just half a dozen raw recruits to guard a shipment like this, do you? And remember, all of you, leave the engineers and that soldier on the locomotive. I need them.'

Halleran made to ask why that particular soldier should be spared, then thought better of it, clamping his lips tightly. No one questioned any decisions Bartell made.

Pushing their way through the deepening snow, they took up their positions, shivering in spite of their heavy clothing.

Despite the rapidly worsening weather, the train was making good progress. There was a number of steep gradients where they were forced to slow as the wheels slipped on the rails. For the most part, however, the line ran straight and level.

Seated with his shoulders against the swaying side of the van, Dave felt the tension inside him beginning to mount. In spite of the sergeant's firm belief that Bartell might not ride out in the storm, he had a distinct sense of unease. He knew something of the outlaw: that he had absconded from the Confederate Army, joining up with men like himself to carry out these daring raids.

The lure of gold and the lust for killing made him

an extremely dangerous and unpredictable enemy. The fact that he had evaded capture for so long also testified to his audacity. Dave felt certain that Bartell would make a try for the gold they were carrying. Somewhere along the line the outlaw was waiting, ready to hit them without any warning.

He got to his feet and moved towards the door, shielding his eyes against the whirling snow as he peered along the line. Here, the terrain was flat, lying under a blanket of white. There was no place along this stretch of the railroad where anyone could conceal himself.

He relaxed a little and withdrew his head. Almost an hour had passed since they had pulled out of Coulson. He knew something of the territory they had to pass through before the train reached its final destination at Fort Amersham.

Felder Rapids, where they might have to stop to take on more fuel and water, was another two hours away. Somehow, it seemed unlikely any attempt would be made there. Bartell was no fool. He had always chosen some place out in the open, well away from any town where a posse might be sent after him.

That left two possible places. Some ten miles further on, the railroad ran through a long, narrow cutting hemmed in on both sides by high walls of rock. There, it would be easy to block the line with boulders and trap the train within the defile.

The only other place was a further fifteen miles on, where a narrow bridge spanned a deep gorge. From what he could recall there was also plenty of cover there on both sides of the track.

He took out paper and tobacco, rolled a cigarette, lit it, and drew the smoke deeply into his lungs. It was going to be a long night. He hoped those soldiers would stand their ground and fight if Bartell struck. If they panicked, it could mean the end for all of them. Less than half an hour later he felt the train beginning to slow and knew the narrow cutting was coming up. He rose swiftly to his feet and leaned out of the narrow opening, slitting his eyes against the snow. For a moment tears threatened to blind him and he brushed them away with the back of his sleeve.

The tall rocks gradually became visible, looming out of the darkness. Hefting the Colts in a tight-fisted grip, he braced himself against the rocking motion of the train. Within two minutes they had entered the downgrade. The wail of the whistle reached him, echoing from the rock walls.

At any second, he expected to hear the screech of the brakes as the engineers spotted some obstruction on the track but the train kept moving, gradually picking up speed again. Slowly, he let his breath go through his mouth. As they came out of the cutting he eased himself back into the shelter of the van. At least, he mused, that settled one question for him. Now he was certain that, somehow, Bartell had obtained a quantity of explosive and that the bridge over the gorge was no longer there.

For a moment, he debated whether to work his way along the outside of the train to warn the engineers, then decided against such a course. If he was right, Bartell wouldn't want the train to go tumbling to the bottom of the gorge into the river. That way, he would lose all of the gold. Clearly, he was banking on the engineers spotting it in time to apply the brakes and bring the train to a halt.

One thing the outlaw hadn't taken into account, however, was this raging blizzard which had struck without warning and was reducing visibility almost to zero. If Bartell had gone ahead with his plan, it meant he was somehow certain the train would be able to stop in time.

He felt a sudden tightness as a fresh thought struck him. Sergeant Rutlidge had asked for someone to ride on the locomotive and Cleaver had immediately volunteered. If the corporal was the one in cahoots with Bartell, he would know exactly what the outlaw intended to do and where he meant to carry it out. Without giving himself away, he could make sure the engineers halted the train in time.

Dave ran the idea through his mind several times and each time it seemed more plausible. It was even possible that, by some means, the corporal was able to obtain the information regarding these shipments and pass it along to Bartell. If there was an attack, he decided it would be a good idea to keep a close eye on Cleaver.

Caution was uppermost in Dave's mind as the train slowed to take a wide curve in the track. Less than half a mile away, the canyon cut a deep slash beneath the railroad. Deep inside, he had been expecting it when the sharp squeal of brakes being hastily applied reached him. With an effort, he steadied himself as the van swayed violently from side to side.

Two minutes later, the locomotive came to a halt and the sound of men shouting reached him from near the front of the train. Swiftly, he eased the door fully open. From the edge of his vision, he was just able to make out the dark, caped figures of the soldiers lowering themselves on to the track. Then the crash of gunfire erupted in the distance. Two of the men dropped instantly and lay unmoving on the snow.

Jumping down from the van, Dave hit the ground hard, rolled over, and came to his feet in a single movement. The gun-flashes from among the rocks bordering the track were just visible in the snow-laden darkness. He guessed there were three men holed up there, keeping their heads down. The sharp staccato of more shots from the other side of the train reached him as he ran forward, doubled over. Weaving from side to side, he threw himself down against the boulders.

The sergeant's loud voice came to him from the distance as the other ordered his men to take cover beneath the wagons. Before they could do so, a further three were hit, tumbling to their knees before they could bring their rifles to bear.

It was soon evident that all of the soldiers were effectively pinned down by the gunmen among the rocks. Unless he could do something to draw the outlaws' fire, all of those men would be slaughtered. Moving like a shadow, he edged among the rocks, keeping his head low.

So far, it seemed that Bartell's men were unaware of his presence. Clearly, they were expecting only soldiers to guard that gold. Less than a minute later he came upon a narrow gully leading up to the top. Carefully, he pulled himself up it, his feet slipping on the layer of ice beneath the snow. His fingers were now so numb there was scarcely any sensation left in them as he used his elbows to draw himself up.

On reaching the top he lifted his head slowly, an inch at a time. Glancing around, he could make out no sign of the outlaws. Then, a vaguely seen shape moved slightly some ten feet from him. Swiftly, Dave lifted his Colt and squeezed off a shot. He saw the man's head jerk back and fall to one side.

It was impossible to tell whether the bullet had found its mark but there was no further movement. The vicious shriek of slugs ricocheting off the rocks dangerously close to his head forced him to crouch down even further. Some of the soldiers had evidently spotted him and in their panic had mistaken him for one of Bartell's men.

Cursing under his breath, he wormed his way another couple of feet along the ridge. A moment later, he came upon the body of the man he had hit. One glance was sufficient to tell him the other was dead. From the man's features, his lips drawn back in a final grimace, he recognized him as a Mexican.

There came the high-pitched whine of a bullet striking the rocks just above his head but it was impossible to determine from which direction it had come. By now, it seemed likely that Bartell had recognized that someone had worked his way to their rear.

As if to confirm this, a bull-like voice suddenly yelled from the darkness in front of him. 'Pablo?'

When there was no answer, the voice came again, more insistent this time. 'Where the hell are you, Pablo?'

Grinning viciously to himself, Dave thrust his back hard against the rocks, his finger tight on the trigger. He doubted if Bartell would take the risk of coming to see for himself what had happened. The man made too big a target. But if he did, he would be ready for him. From the sound of Bartell's voice, he judged the other to be less than ten feet away, concealed somewhere within the tumbled mass of boulders which showed as vague shapes through the driving snow.

Down below, the soldiers, although still outnumbering the outlaws, were fighting a losing battle. Caught in the open, they were being cut down one by one by the accurate fire from the rocks. Only six now remained alive, trapped inside the van, unable to show themselves. The rest lay strewn on the snow beside the train.

The crash of gunfire continued unabated but judging from the volume of the return rifle fire, Dave guessed it would soon be over for those men unless he could get Bartell. Cautiously, he eased himself away from the rockface. There came a sudden soft sound at his back, the scrape of a boot on rock. Whirling, he tried to bring up his gun. He had just sufficient time to glimpse the dark shape, to see the upraised arm, before the gun-butt struck him on the back of the head, pitching him headlong down the steep slope.

*

Standing by the side of the track, Bartell surveyed the scene in front of him with a broad grin of satisfaction on his fleshy features. He had never doubted his plan would succeed. Now fourteen men lay dead, most of them on the snow near the train, the others inside the van.

He turned as Halleran came towards him, dragging Dave's unconscious form through the snow. Allowing the inert body to drop limply in front of Bartell, the other said hoarsely: 'He killed Pablo, Ned. Reckon he's a federal marshal. I spotted the star on his shirt. What the hell was he doin' with the train?'

Bartell bent and turned Dave's body over. 'I know this man,' he growled. 'His name's Stevens. He's been after me for years.' He glanced up sharply. 'You didn't kill him?'

Halleran shook his head. 'I just cracked his skull a little. I figured you might want to talk with him before we shoot him.'

Bartell rubbed the snow from his eyes, shaking his head. 'I ain't interested in talkin' to him, but I want him alive.' There was a crafty gleam in his small, deep-set eyes. 'I've got another plan for him. He's been a thorn in my hide for too long. Guess it's about time to put a finish to it. But I'm goin' to let the Army do it for me.'

He looked round as Cleaver climbed down from the locomotive, his rifle covering the two engineers. Leaving them beside the locomotive, he walked over.

'It seems everythin' went accordin' to plan, Ned,' he said tersely. 'What do we do with those two men?' His glance suddenly took in Stevens's body lying in the snow. 'That's the marshal who got on the train at Coulson with us. I was a bit worried when the commandant allowed him to travel with the train.'

'Well, you won't have to worry about him any more. Once we get that gold loaded on to the wagon, you come with us. It won't be safe for you to go back. The Army will soon start askin' how you came to be the only one left alive.'

'And him?' Cleaver prodded Dave with his boot. 'You leavin' him here? That would be a fool thing to do. If he was to talk we would have the whole o' the Army and a dozen federal marshals on our tails. There'd be no place to hide.'

Bartell paused to check that the heavy boxes of gold were being stacked into the waiting wagon. Then he said ferally: 'It won't make any difference if he does talk. Nobody will believe him after tonight.'

'What makes you so goddamned sure o' that?'

'Because they're goin' to find enough evidence on him to connect him with us, certainly enough to hang him. They'll believe he's the one who's been supplyin' us with this information. You'll be in the clear.'

He jerked a thumb towards the wagon. 'Open one o' those boxes and bring me a couple o' those gold bars.'

Cleaver returned a few moments later and handed the gold to Bartell. Bending, the other placed them inside Dave's jacket, drawing it tightly around them, making sure the engineers saw nothing.

'Now what do we do?' Cleaver asked as Bartell straightened with a grunt.

In answer, the other called to the rest of the men. 'Get all o' those bodies into the van, together with this one. Then have those engineers lock the door and take this train back to Coulson.'

CHAPTER II

ACCUSATION!

Dave's return to consciousness was a slow and painful process, He was lying on something hard in utter darkness and there was a swaying motion which he could not understand. Then, slowly, fragments of memory came back. He recalled hearing Bartell's loud voice calling orders to his men. Then that man who had crept up on him from behind and slugged him with a gun-butt. After that, there was nothing.

With an effort, he pushed himself into a sitting position, struggling to control the nausea in his stomach and the pain which lanced agonizingly through his skull with every movement. He had no idea how long he had been out but he guessed it must have been for several hours. As for those men guarding the train, he knew nothing of what had happened to the survivors if, indeed, there were any.

Reaching up, he felt the back of his head. There was dried blood on his scalp and in his hair. Sucking in a racking breath that hurt his chest, he suddenly realized there was something heavy and bulky beneath his jacket.

Fumbling awkwardly, he ran his numbed fingers over the two objects, tracing their shape with his hands in the blackness. Long and oblong, it took him several moments to recognize what they were. Gold bars!

Desperately, he forced himself to think clearly. Why would Bartell go to all the trouble to leave these? he wondered. The answer, when it came to him in a flash of clarity, sent a warning tingle along his spine. The outlaw intended to frame him as his accomplice in this hold-up!

Bracing himself against the side of the van, still unsteady on his feet, he pushed himself upright. The rattle of the wheels on the track hammered painfully through his head as he slowly worked his way towards the door. On the way, he stumbled over something heavy. Bending, he felt the body lying on the floor.

There was no sound from the man and he guessed the other was dead. Striking a match, he held it out in front of him, trying to make out details in the feeble yellow glow. There were other bodies in the van, lying on the floor where they had been thrown.

Fighting to maintain his balance, he reached the door only to find that it had been securely locked from the outside.

All of his thinking was bleak as he realized how well the outlaw had planned everything. He had no idea where the train was heading. Certainly, with that bridge destroyed, the only way they could go was back in the direction of Coulson. Evidently, Bartell had deliberately spared the lives of the two engineers rather than kill them out of hand as was his usual custom.

That fact merely confirmed his suspicion that once he had showed up on the train, he had given the outlaw the perfect opportunity to identify him as the one responsible for providing those killers with vital information. There was no point in hiding it on one of the dead men. Once found, that would immediately point to his guilt.

The abrupt deceleration ten minutes later, followed by the thin screech of brakes, told him they must be approaching their destination. Placing his hands on the side of the van, he leaned his weight on them and waited until the train came to a halt.

A few moments later, he picked out the sound of voices outside and then the rattle of a key in the lock. The door slid open and he saw one of the engineers standing just below him on the platform. The other started back in shocked surprise, then controlled himself and reached up a hand to help Dave down.

'We thought everybody in there was dead, Marshal,' he stuttered. 'I saw those outlaws load all of the bodies inside and thought—'

'Never mind about that,' Dave said sharply. 'Where is this place?'

'We're back in Coulson,' the other replied. 'Those killers ordered us to bring the train back. We only just made it with the fuel we had on board.'

'Is there any place here where you can get a message through to the Army post?'

The other glanced round. 'Maybe in the office yonder but it's all locked up for the night.'

'Then smash the door down,' Dave ordered. 'This is urgent. Tell whoever is in charge to get some men here as soon as possible.'

Waiting inside the office once the call had gone through, Dave tried desperately to put his thoughts into a coherent order. He still felt groggy although the pain in his head was gradually subsiding. The second engineer came back from his inspection of the van. His face looked ashen under the smoke and grime and there was a haunted look in his eyes.

'All of 'em shot,' he muttered thinly. 'It must have been a wholesale massacre. They never really had a chance, cut down before they could get out o' that van and under cover.'

He looked down at the gold bars on the small table and then across at Dave. There was now a curious expression on his face. 'Why the hell did they leave these?'

'I found 'em stuffed inside my jacket when I came round,' Dave explained. He saw by the way both men looked at him that they, too, were turning over in their minds the possibility that he was the informer.

Neither man said anything more after that. One of them walked to the door and then made his way out of sight along the platform.

It was more than half an hour later when the sound of horses outside the depot heralded the arrival of men from the army post. There were six of them, led by an efficient-looking lieutenant.

After sending four of the men along the train to

the van, the lieutenant walked over to Dave. His face was completely expressionless as he said: 'I'm Lieutenant Roger Delmore, United States Cavalry. I believe you are Federal Marshal Stevens.'

'That's right, Lieutenant.' Dave gave a brief nod. 'I had permission from your commandant to travel with the train.'

'I've no doubt the major will want to question you, Marshal,' Delmore said. He seated himself in the chair at the table. 'From what little I know, the train was attacked by this outlaw, Bartell.' His gaze bored into Dave and his harsh voice contained barely controlled fury. 'How the hell did this happen? We were supposed to be ready for them. Now we've lost a good sergeant and fifteen men.'

'Fourteen men, Lieutenant,' Dave replied, forcing evenness into his tone. 'If you examine those bodies, you'll find that Corporal Cleaver isn't among them.'

Delmore's eyes narrowed at that remark. He made to say something, then stopped as two of the soldiers returned.

'They're all dead, sir,' said one of them tonelessly.

'Is Corporal Cleaver's body among them?' Delmore demanded.

'No, sir.' The second soldier spoke up. 'It could be he was killed like the others and his body was left behind.'

Rubbing his numbed hands together, Dave interrupted. 'My guess is that he's still alive.'

Delmore considered that and then. shook his head emphatically. 'Somehow, I doubt that. He'd have made it back to the train after those outlaws rode out with the gold. Cleaver was a good soldier.'

'There's one other possibility,' Dave went on thinly.

'Oh?' The lieutenant glanced up in surprise. 'What might that be, Marshal?'

'Someone was passing information about these shipments to Bartell, someone who knew when these trains were leaving and from which depot. If it was Cleaver, he'll be somewhere out there with Bartell and his gang by now.'

Delmore's lean features twisted into a scowl. Hammering with his fist on the table, he rasped: 'That is something I do not believe. I know the men under my command. I picked them myself for this mission.'

His glance suddenly fell on the two gold bars. 'Where did these come from?'

One of the engineers spoke up before Dave could answer. 'According to the marshal here, he found them in his jacket when he regained consciousness inside the van.'

The lieutenant was silent for several moments. When he spoke again there was a heightened note of suspicion in his voice. 'I reckon you'll have a heap of explainin' to do once we get you back to the post, Marshal.'

Dave felt a sudden surge of fury pass through him at the other's remark. Somehow, he managed to fight it down as he replied tightly, 'If you're suggestin' I had anything to do with this attack, Lieutenant, you couldn't be more wrong. I've been on Bartell's trail even longer than the Army. I went with that train to bring him back, dead or alive and if you think—'

'It's not what I think, Marshal,' Delmore retorted acidly. 'You'll get your chance to defend yourself in front of Major Cauldwell. Right now, I'm confiscating this gold and takin' you back with me, together with those bodies for burial.'

Dave knew that any further argument would be useless. Delmore held out his hands. 'Until all of this has been sorted out, I'll take your guns, Marshal.'

Reluctantly, Dave handed them over, aware that the two soldiers in the doorway had their hands close to their rifles. He knew they would use them instantly if the lieutenant gave the command.

On the platform, the other soldiers were carrying the dead men from the van out to the street, where Dave guessed there were wagons waiting to take them to the army post. Inwardly, he felt a white-hot blaze of fury against Bartell. By now, the outlaw was probably laughing at the way he had turned the tables against him.

Gritting his teeth, he swore that somehow, he would hunt the outlaw down even if he had to track him all the way clear to the California border. Before that, however, he had to convince the major that he was telling the truth: that Cleaver was the traitor in their ranks.

It was still early morning when the small detachment reached the army post. While the dead were taken from the wagons to the mortuary; Delmore ordered Dave down and marched him towards a long, low building with iron bars across the three windows.

Here, he was placed in one of the cells.

'When do I get to see the major?' Dave asked as the lieutenant prepared to move away.

'He'll see you when he comes on duty in a few hours,' the other replied tersely. 'If you want my advice, you'll get some sleep.'

Stretching himself out on the low iron bed, Dave clasped his hands behind his neck and stared at the low ceiling. The bleeding on his scalp had stopped. Now there was merely a dull ache, a persistent throbbing which made it difficult to think clearly.

Almost before he knew it, he was asleep. When he woke it was to find a soldier standing beside the bed. He had a tray of food and some water which he handed to Dave. There was another man with a rifle in the passage outside the cell.

'What time is it?' he asked as the man turned away.

'A quarter after eight,' the other replied. 'Better get that eaten, you'll be seein' the commandant in an hour.'

Dave ate ravenously. It seemed ages since he had last eaten a proper meal. When he was finished, he waited until Lieutenant Delmore appeared. There were two armed men with him. Evidently, Dave thought, they were taking no chances on him escaping.

Major Cauldwell was a short, hawk-faced man with piercing blue eyes that drilled into Dave as he entered the office. His greying hair gave his age as somewhere in the sixties but he still held himself as stiff as a ramrod in his chair.

Motioning to the chair in front of his desk, he

glanced in the direction of the lieutenant standing just inside the doorway. 'That will be all, Lieutenant,' he said sharply. 'This is not a court martial.'

For a moment, a look of disappointment flashed over Delmore's features but it was gone in an instant. Saluting, he went out, closing the door behind him.

Cauldwell stared down at some scribbled notes on a piece of paper in front of him. His expression was inscrutable. At last he looked up. 'Perhaps I should hear your side of the story, Stevens, before I reach any judgment.' He indicated the two gold blocks on the desk. 'You don't deny these were found on you when that train arrived back in Caulson?'

'No, I admitted that to the lieutenant at the depot. It's quite obvious Bartell put them there to incriminate me.'

Cauldwell placed the tips of his fingers together and waited for him to go on. Briefly, Dave told what had happened after the train had been brought to a halt. The major listened attentively, not once interrupting until Dave had finished.

At the end he sat forward in his chair, placing his elbows on the desk. 'I suppose you realize just how much evidence there is against you. Frankly, I was against allowing you to accompany that train. I've known for some time that someone has been working with this outlaw, providing him with accurate details of our movement of gold consignments.

'Admittedly, I fail to see how you could have had access to these details, yet it's something I can't rule out. However, I should tell you that I gave orders for that train to return to the scene of the attack to search for Corporal Cleaver's body.'

'Did you find it?'

Cauldwell shook his head. 'No, we didn't, in spite of an extensive search of the area.'

'Then surely that points to him bein' the one in cahoots with Bartell. I certainly didn't knock myself out and then climb into that van. I was deliberately put there to throw suspicion away from Cleaver. If I was workin' for Bartell, he wouldn't send me back with incriminatin' evidence on me.'

Cauldwell picked up his pen and twirled it between his fingers. 'Sometimes, it's difficult to get into a mind like Bartell's.'

Dave changed the subject slightly. 'Did you have any suspicions about Cleaver? Could he have had access to this kind of information?'

'It's possible. As for my suspicions, I suspect everyone. One thing I am certain of – if he is the man, he wasn't working alone.'

Dave raised his brows a little and tried to read the expression on the major's face. 'What makes you say that?'

'Even if Cleaver got the information, there's no way he could send it to Bartell without arousing suspicion.'

'I see.' Dave paused, then said: 'From the way you're talking', telling me all this, I gather you don't think I had anythin' to do with these hold-ups.'

Cauldwell hesitated momentarily, then nodded. 'I've checked on you, Marshal. From what I've been told, you're a straight-shooter. That's why I wanted to speak to you alone. The Army has had no success in apprehending this outlaw. We lost a lot of good men yesterday and I can't afford to lose any more. In my mind, you're the best hope we have of getting Bartell and his band.'

Dave let his breath go in little pinches through his teeth. 'I guess you know I've been on his trail for almost four years but he's always given me the slip. I also know the Army wants him as much as I do, but I get the feelin' it's for somethin' more than just these robberies.'

The major pursed his lips into a thin line, a speculative expression in his eyes. Then he leaned forward and said softly: 'The Union Army only wants him for that gold. You may know that during the war, he served with the Confederates. He sold a lot of their secrets to us. In other words he was a traitor to his cause. Some two thousand of their troops were ambushed and killed because of what he told us. That was when he went on the run and there are still plenty of men in this territory who can't forget that.'

Sitting back, Dave digested the major's words. No one, no matter on which side they had fought, would have any liking for a traitor. Selling information about gold-shipments was one thing but the wholesale slaughter of so many men was a totally different matter.

Glancing up, he said: 'You can rely on me to do everythin' I can to bring him in, Major. It ain't goin' to be easy. He's got someplace where he can hole up and—'

Interrupting, Cauldwell cut in: 'I may be able to give you a little help. I presume you've heard of the

Pinkerton Agency.'

'Some. I've never had any dealings with them.'

'They seem to think that Bartell has a hideout somewhere close to a place called Sioux Falls. It's a small frontier town some two hundred miles west. One of their agents is working there at the moment. I suggest you get in touch with her. She may be able to provide you with some vital information.'

Dave tried to suppress his sense of surprise. 'A woman!'

What passed for a smile flashed across the other's stem features. 'They do sometimes employ women in their operations.' He scribbled something on a piece of paper and handed it across the desk. 'This is her name. She works as a singer in the Lost Trail saloon.' He paused, then continued: 'One more thing. I would remove that star before you get there. From the reports I've received, Sioux Falls is one hell of a town. Don't trust the sheriff or his deputy.'

Dave glanced at the paper in his hand. 'Marie Devlin.'

'Perhaps I should tell you that she has a very good reason for wanting Bartell dead. Her brother was among those soldiers killed during that ambush.'

Cauldwell got stiffly to his feet, holding out his hand. 'Good luck, Marshal. This time I hope you're successful. There's just one other thing which may help. I've spoken with your superiors. There'll be word that you were shot by my men while trying to escape. It may make Bartell careless if he thinks you're no longer on his trail.'

*

Bartell and his men had ridden swiftly through the night, swinging away from the railroad and heading south across the mesa into the teeth of the blinding storm. In spite of the atrocious weather, Bartell was feeling highly pleased at the way things had turned out. It was true he had lost one of his men, but that represented no problem. He could always bring in more men from across the border to replace him.

Pushing his mount forward until he was riding alongside the wagon, Halleran leaned sideways in the saddle and yelled: 'You goin' to stash the gold in the same place as always, Ned?'

Bartell's lips curled into a sneer. 'The gold goes in the one place where I know it's safe. So long as only one of us knows where it is, nobody else can talk if they get caught.'

Halleran shook his head and brushed away the snow which fell from his hat. 'Nope, I guess not.'

Leaning forward on the traces, Bartell flicked the whip across the back of the straining horse. He was now anxious to get out of the storm which still showed no sign of abating. He knew that when the weather turned bad like this, such blizzards could last for days and the sooner they reached their destination, the better he would feel.

Up ahead, some three miles away, lay the pass. If that were blocked by snow, it would mean a long ride along the range of hills, which could add a further two or three hours to their journey. He also had one further problem on his mind, one which he had known about for some time.

That gold they had taken from the two previous

hold-ups was concealed in a place known only to himself. He knew the others didn't like it, but so far his word had been law. It was quite possible they no longer trusted him and, with all that gold in the wagon behind him, they might forget about the gold they had already taken and decide to kill him, dividing it among themselves rather than wait until he decided they had enough.

It was only the fact that his plans had succeeded so well that kept them together but sooner or later they would get tired of waiting. Now, as he rode on the swaying traces of the wagon, he held the reins tightly in his left fist and kept his right hand close to his gun. It was unlikely they would try anything before they got out of this storm and reached Sioux Falls. But he was taking no chances.

An hour later, by the time they came within five miles of the town, the snow slackened. There were just a few flakes whirling in the wind. Over towards the east, a grey, dismal dawn was breaking.

Hauling the wagon to a halt, he called harshly: 'The rest o' you men ride into town and wait for me. I'll put this gold with the rest and—'

'It seems to us we've already got more'n enough to last us for the rest of our lives.' Halleran called back. 'Sooner or later our luck is goin' to run out. I say we ride with you to where you've got the rest stashed and share it out now.'

'Do you now?' Bartell's voice was low but filled with menace. 'And who appointed you the leader o' this band?' He turned his head slowly, a look of smouldering fury on his features. 'Any o' you others feel the same way?'

'Perhaps what Señor Halleran says makes sense,' Meninguez put in. 'It will not be long before the Army sends more men and with Cleaver here no longer able to supply us with information, we could—'

Reaching to his left so quickly the eye could scarcely follow the movement, Bartell grasped the whip. His hand scarcely seemed to move as it lashed out, the tip drawing a streak of blood across the Mexican's cheek.

'We finish when I say we do,' Bartell snarled as the other reeled sideways in the saddle, his hand going up to his face. 'Now all o' you get into town. We'll meet again in the saloon. If you've got any other ideas, I suggest you go for your guns right now.'

When there was no further dissent, he sat back and watched as they rode off. His brooding gaze continued to follow them until they had vanished into the distance. He knew they would obey him for a time but a little voice at the back of his mind warned him that greedy men could be dangerous.

He brought the whip down across the horse's back, turned the wagon and headed east. Just so long as none of them knew exactly where the gold was hidden, he was safe. They needed him alive for that information.

There was a cruel amusement on his face as he headed the wagon towards the range of low hills which just showed on the misty horizon. He had come upon the old Indian village some three years earlier: just a handful of adobe huts in a small clearing on the hillside. By the look of it, he had guessed it had been abandoned several decades earlier and he doubted if anyone in Sioux Falls even knew of its existence.

He continually threw watchful glances over his shoulder, making certain he was not being followed. He was absolutely certain that none of the men who rode with him was aware of the place where he kept the gold. It stood well inside the forest and there were now no tracks leading to it. Over the years, these had become overgrown with thick brush until they were completely obliterated. There was, however, a narrow Indian track leading over the hills but this passed no closer than a mile of it.

By the time he reached the hills a watery sun had risen, throwing everything into light and shadow. Cautiously, he guided the horse along the narrow track.

It was heavy going. Long, wiry tendrils snaked across his path and Spanish sword slashed at his clothing as he urged the animal onward. At last, however, he came out on to the small plateau where the remains of the small settlement stood. It was unusual for the Indians to build their adobes among the hills and trees; usually they preferred the wide, open plains, but he guessed they had done this to escape from the white man when he had invaded their territory.

He took up the shovel he had brought with him and entered one of the ruins. It took almost half an hour for him to dig the large hole in the hard, earthen floor. By the time he had finished he was sweating profusely in spite of the chill in the air. After he had lowered the boxes into it, he returned for the remainder. Then he filled in the hole and stamped it down with his boots.

Not until he was satisfied that no one could tell that the floor had been disturbed did he lead the horse and wagon back down the hillside and head in the direction of Sioux Falls.

The town was coming alive as he rode in, heading along the narrow street towards the livery stables. Here, he left the horse and wagon with the groom and then headed for the saloon. His four companions were already there, seated at one of the tables in the corner.

Signalling to the bartender, he walked over and lowered himself into the empty chair.

'You have it all well hidden, Señor Bartell?' Meninguez asked softly.

Bartell gave a cursory nod. 'It's all been taken care of,' he retorted thinly. 'It's where no one but me can find it.' He saw the looks that passed among the seated men but pretended not to notice them.

'So what's the plan now?' Woodrow asked.

Bartell waited while the bartender brought a bottle and glass, placing them on the table in front of him. When the other had moved away, he said: 'We lie low for a while. I ain't expecting any trouble but there's no point in takin' chances.'

Cleaver finished his drink and poured more whiskey into his glass. Without looking up, he said: 'You ain't thinking o' making any more raids, are you, Ned? By now the Army will have figured out that

I gave you that information. The sooner I get rid o' this uniform, the better.'

Easing his bulk more comfortably in the chair, Bartell muttered: 'You're right. Even in Sioux Falls, folk could get mighty suspicious if they was to see a soldier ridin' with us.'

CHAPTER III

SIOUX FALLS

Two days later, an hour before dawn, Dave was in the saddle, heading west across a flat, barren terrain. A deep, empty stillness lay like a shadow over this sullen country. He had encountered a number of trails, running alongside the railroad, where wagon trains had headed this way, looking for the rich lands of Southern California.

Here and there he had come upon wrecked skeletons of large wagons, lying on their sides, and small groups of crude wooden crosses in the sand which marked the final resting-places of those who hadn't made this crossing. Ever since the railroad had spanned this territory, there had been fewer and fewer of them and he guessed that whatever had happened to these wagon trains, it had been many years before.

He had reached the gorge the previous afternoon. Apart from the remnants of the bridge there was little to show of the massacre. Some day soon the engineers would come out to rebuild the bridge. Whatever happened, the railroad had to go on.

At this point, he had turned south, following the winding course of the canyon. Much of the snow had now gone, leaving the ground thick with mud. He had deliberately allowed his mount its head, relying upon it to find the safest places. When night had fallen, he had found a deep hollow, screened from the bitter wind by a stand of stunted trees, making cold camp.

He had gone along with Major Cauldwell's plan and now there was no star beneath his jacket. To any stranger, he was just another drifter, apparently on the run from the law. Lifting his head to scan the region just ahead of him, he noticed the dark smudge, perhaps a quarter of a mile away, and headed towards it.

It was a series of low ridges with gnarled bushes growing out of the arid soil at their bases. He was less than 200 yards away when his mount suddenly shied. For a moment, he thought the horse had detected a rattler. Then, from the edge of his vision, he detected the spurt of rifle fire.

Instinct took over as he threw himself sideways from the saddle, hitting the ground hard and rolling over. The heavy Colt in his right hand, he slithered swiftly away from the stallion. Without lifting his body from the ground, he used his legs to slide forward on his stomach until he reached the thick bushes.

Crouching down, he waited. A few moments later,

a shadowy figure emerged from the rocks and edged towards the horse. Dave waited until the man was less than a few yards away; then rose silently to his feet. The barrel of the Colt was lined on the other's back.

'Just take it easy, friend, and drop that rifle,' he said softly. 'I don't want to kill you, but I will if you make any wrong move.'

He saw the other stiffen. For an instant, the man's shoulder dropped a fraction, as if he intended to take his chances and make his play. Then, slowly, he released his grip on the weapon and let it fall to the ground at his feet.

'Now turn round – slowly.'

The man turned to face him. He was a tall man of middle age with rough, angular features. The unruly hair showing beneath his hat was grey and sparse. To Dave he didn't look like a cold-blooded killer but in these parts that went for nothing.

'Now maybe you'll tell me why you tried to kill me,' Dave said, his voice ominously low. The other's lips drew back across his teeth. He wore twin Colts but he kept his hands well away from the guns. His voice was a harsh snarl as he rasped: 'Go ahead, killer. Shoot me down, because I ain't goin' back to Sioux Falls.'

Not once relaxing his vigilance, Dave said tautly: 'I've got no call to kill you, mister. If I had, you'd be dead by now. And I sure don't aim to take you back to Sioux Falls.'

Dave holstered the Colt, confident that the other would make no more trouble. He saw some of the suspicion fade from the other's face. 'But you ain't answered my question. Why did you try to bushwhack me?'

'Guess I owe you an apology, friend. I had you figured for one o' Bender's men.'

'Bender?'

'That's right. Jesse Bender. He runs most o' Sioux Falls. Some folk reckon he's in with that outlaw, Bartell and his gang.' The other must have seen the expression of interest which crossed Dave's faced, for he went on; 'You know this *hombre*, Bender?'

Dave shook his head. 'Never heard of him,' he replied. 'But anythin' to do with Bartell and his band I make my business. What's your name, mister?'

'Carlton, Ben Carlton. I own a small spread not far from the town. But if you've got a score to settle with Bartell, I'd ride clear o' Sioux Falls, Mister—?'

'Dave Stevens.' He motioned to the gun lying on the ground. 'Pick up your weapon, Carlton. Let's just call what happened back there a little misunderstanding.' He waited as the other bent and picked up the Winchester. 'If you have a ranch close by, why ain't you there?'

'Had some steers rustled a couple o' nights back,' explained Carlton. 'Since then I've been keepin' a look-out for those coyotes. I reckoned you might have been one of 'em. That's why I took a shot at you.'

He moved a little closer to Dave. 'I guess you could do with some grub.' Noticing the dust on Dave's jacket, he remarked: 'Now I get a close look at you, I figure you've ridden quite a ways.'

'Reckon I could use somethin' to eat. I've been in the saddle all the way from Coulson.'

'Coulson? Hell, that's a couple o' hundred miles east. Get your mount and I'll take you back to my place.'

Saddling up, Dave rode alongside as the older man headed away from the canyon. Gradually, the country changed. The barren aridness gave way to pasture land. Soon they came upon a stout fence which clearly marked the perimeter of Carlton's spread.

Carlton dismounted, unlocked the large gate and pushed it open, motioning Dave through, before closing it behind him. A narrow track led over a low hill. Down below, Dave made out the herd with a couple of rim-riders circling it in the growing light.

A mile further on they entered a wide courtyard fronting a small ranch house. Carlton led him inside, motioning him to a chair at the table. Ten minutes later he came in from the kitchen with two heaped plates of eggs, bacon and beans. There was also a jug of hot coffee.

While he ate, Dave plied the other with questions. 'You know any place around here where the Bartell gang can hide out?'

'Hide out?' Carlton grinned. 'There ain't any need for 'em to hide out here. They walk the streets in broad daylight. You'll find 'em in the Yellow Ridge or the Lost Trail saloons most days.'

'And the law does nothin' about it?'

Carlton shook his head, chewing slowly on his food. 'There's only one law in Sioux Falls and that's

Jesse Bender. He owns most o' the land, the saloons and the bank. Guess it's like this in any frontier town you care to mention. These are lawless days this far west.'

Taking a couple of swallows of his coffee, he paused, then went on harshly: 'It only takes one man with an army o' hired gunmen at his back. Bender came to this town some two years ago from some place way out East. Now he's the law, judge and jury. Anyone who tries to go against him ends up on Boot Hill.'

'And where does Bartell fit in? He never struck me as a man who'd take orders from anyone.'

Laying down his knife and fork, Carlton hesitated a moment before replying. 'Bartell's a wanted man. They say he's wanted both by the law and a lot o' those who fought on the Confederate side durin' the war. But he's got somethin' Bender wants more than anything else – gold.

'Bender knows that Bartell has more gold hidden away somewhere in this territory than you could ever imagine. My guess is that's he's aiming to get his hands on all of it. But Bartell's clever. He's the only one who knows where that gold is stashed. None o' those killers ridin' with him knows where it is.'

Dave poured himself more coffee and rolled a cigarette. He lit it and inhaled deeply. It was indeed fortunate he had met up with Carlton. It was clear the other knew a great deal about what was happening in Sioux Falls.

A few moments later there was the sound of riders approaching. Carlton jerked himself tautly erect in his chair, throwing a swift glance towards the window.

'Some of your boys?' Dave asked.

Carlton shook his head. 'They won't be ridin' in at this time unless there's been trouble with the herd.' His tone was hard and incisive. Getting swiftly to his feet, he crossed to the window and glanced out.

'It's Bender and three of his gunhawks.' He grabbed the Winchester lying against the wall. 'You'd better stay out o' this,' he muttered thinly.

He opened the door and stepped outside on to the veranda, holding the rifle by his side. 'What the hell do you want, Bender?' he called loudly.

Moving swiftly to the window, Dave saw the tall, thin man dressed in a black frock-coat. A thin moustache drooped across his upper lip and there was a faintly derisive smile on his pursed lips. He leaned forward, resting one elbow on the saddle horn.

'You know why I'm here, Carlton. I made you a damned good offer for this land a couple o' days ago. Seems to me you've had plenty o' time to consider it.'

'The answer's the same as it was two days ago. I don't aim to sell either the land or the herd.'

Bender's features hardened, his angular cheeks drawn down tightly, his brows knitted into a hard line. 'Now I reckon that's mighty unneighbourly of you. From what I've heard you've only four men to help you on this spread. How long do you reckon you can go on without more help?'

'Long enough,' Carlton retorted. 'I know how you work, Bender. Get some o' your men to rustle our cattle; then move in and try to buy us out at a quarter of what the spreads are worth.'

Bender's eyes narrowed to slits as he drew himself up. 'Now I sure hope you ain't accusin' me, or any o' my men, of rustling, Carlton. Sheriff Mawson might not take too kindly to that unless you got some proof.'

'He's got no proof, Jesse,' cut in one of the riders. 'He's just full o' talk. Reckon if we were to have a word with his hired men they'd soon see it'd be healthy for 'em to ride on.'

'You don't frighten me none,' Carlton said sharply, a trace of defiance in his tone.

'No?' Before Carlton could raise the Winchester, the gunhawk had pulled his Colt, aiming it at the rancher. 'Guess if I was to put a bullet into your leg, you might find it more difficult to—'

The gunslinger's words were cut off abruptly, as the single gunshot echoed across the courtyard. The man uttered a yell of agony, clutching at his hand as his Colt went spinning into the dirt.

Stepping through the door, Dave said softly: 'I guess you didn't hear what my friend said. He ain't selling this place. Now unless any more of you want to make a play for your guns, I suggest you turn your mounts and ride out o' here.'

A red flush spread over Bender's face as he struggled to control his fury. Through tightly clenched teeth, he muttered: 'I don't know who you are, stranger. But you've just made a big mistake. I never forget a face and the next time we meet, you'll be the one to regret it.'

Dave's eyes flicked towards one of the other

gunhawks as the man moved his right hand slightly towards his holster. 'Just try it,' he said evenly. 'It'll be the last thing you do.'

The other's features twisted into a scowl and for a second there was a look of indecision in his close-set eyes. Then he pulled his hand away.

'Now ride back to town,' Carlton said, levelling his Winchester on Bender. 'Better get the doctor to take a look at your hired killer's hand.'

Cursing loudly under his breath, Bender pulled savagely on the reins and wheeled his mount. Over his shoulder, he called harshly: 'You've had your chance, Carlton. Now you're finished.'

Dave watched until the riders had vanished in a dwindling cloud of dust and then followed the rancher into the house.

'You shouldn't have stepped in there, Dave,' Carlton said, seating himself at the table. 'Now you've made a bad enemy o' Bender.'

Dave gave a tight grin. 'I already have an enemy in Bartell. One more won't make much difference.'

He lowered himself into the chair and went on: 'From what you tell me, this man Bender owns the town and he's the law there. That bein' so, the Bartell gang have nothin' to fear from the sheriff in Sioux Falls.'

'That's the way it is. Mawson takes his orders from Bender. You ain't figurin' on riding into town after Bartell? That would be plain suicide. If you're lookin' for a job, you're welcome to work for me. I need men fast with a gun. It won't be long before Bender decides to move against me and—'

'I'd sure like to help you, Ben. But first I have a job to finish.'

'You sure must want Bartell pretty bad to even consider goin' up against him.' Carlton took out a pipe and thrust shreds of tobacco into the bowl. He struck a match and waved it across the pipe, sucking noisily until he had it going to his satisfaction.

Dave got to his feet and crossed to the window, staring out into the courtyard. Without turning his head, he asked: 'Do you go into town often, Ben?'

Surprised at the question, Carlton stared at him through the wreathing of smoke. 'Sometimes. Just for supplies. Why do you ask?'

'You know a woman by the name o' Marie Devlin?'

'Sure I've heard of her. She's the singer at the Lost Trail saloon. Is she a friend o' yours?'

Dave shook his head. 'Nope. I've never met her, but a friend o' mine back in Coulson asked me to look her up.' He went back to the table and stood with his hands on the back of the chair, looking down at Carlton.

Ben grinned up at him. 'From what I've heard, she's one hell of a woman. Bender hired her some months ago. You can't mistake her: red-haired with a temper like a wildcat. She stands no nonsense from any o' the customers. Some folk reckon she's Bender's woman but if you want my opinion, she's her own woman.'

Moving towards the door, Dave said: 'Guess it's time I paid her a visit. Thanks for the meal, Ben.'

Carlton pushed himself from the chair and accompanied him on to the veranda. 'Watch your back in that helltown, Dave. There are men there who'll shoot you in the back without any warnin'. I wouldn't like to see you end up on Boot Hill like so many others who've gone against Bender and Bartell.'

'I'll watch myself.' Dave stepped down into the courtyard and made his way to where his mount was tethered to the rail. Behind him, Carlton called: 'If things don't turn out for you, you're always welcome here.'

'I'll keep that in mind.' He swung into the saddle and set the stallion to a brisk gallop.

Jesse Bender was seething with fury as he thrust open the door of the sheriff's office and stormed inside. Seated behind the desk, Sheriff Mawson instantly jumped to his feet as Bender entered. He was a small man, middle-aged, and running to fat.

'Somethin' wrong, Mr Bender?' His voice quavered a little and he found it impossible to look the taller man in the eye as Bender pulled out a chair and lowered himself into it.

'That damned fool, Carlton. I rode out to make him a final offer for his spread and he laughed in my face.'

Mawson swallowed hard. He knew if he said the wrong thing while Bender was in this foul mood, he would regret it. 'Surely it wouldn't have been difficult for your men to make him see sense. I mean—'

'I did take men with me but he's got some stranger there with him. He looked like some fast gun from across the border. Shot the gun out o' Mike's hand. I've just taken him to the doc. I'm tellin' you, Mawson, I want him off that spread pronto. I don't give a damn how you do it – just see that it's done.'

Mawson sank into his chair. 'I'll get some men together and ride out there right away. But it won't be easy. He's owned that spread for more'n twelve years and he won't go without a fight.'

Bender leaned forward over the desk, his face thrust up close to the sheriff's. 'I pay you to keep the law around here. I'm sure you can think up some reason for gettin' him off that land.'

'I'll do my best, Mr Bender.'

'Then just make sure your best is good enough.' A crafty look momentarily replaced the anger which suffused Bender's features. 'Better make it look like an accident. At the moment, I don't want the rest o' the ranchers banding together against me. There's no way o' tellin' what the rest o' the town might do if that happened.'

He leaned back, locked his fingers together, and stared at the ceiling. 'From what I saw o' that place it's nearly all timber. Now if a fire was to start I guess it wouldn't take long to burn the whole lot down. You get my meanin'?'

Mawson forced a weak grin. 'I understand. And this stranger – what if he should decide to butt in?'

Bender's thin lips curled into a vicious smile. 'I'm sure you can take care of him. I don't like men ridin' into my territory that I know nothin' about. They make me nervous.'

Bender rose smoothly to his feet and went to the door. He paused before opening it. 'You got any idea if Bartell is in town?'

'He was at the Lost Trail saloon half an hour ago. Reckon he might still be there.'

'Good. It's just possible might know something about this gunslinger.'

Bender walked out and made his way along the boardwalk. The saloon was situated halfway along the street, a two-storey building which dominated those on either side of it. He pushed open the doors and went inside.

He spotted Bartell's huge bulk at the table in the far corner. A swift glance told him the rest of the outlaw's men were standing along the bar. He went across and lowered himself into the chair opposite Bartell.

He signalled to the bartender and waited until a bottle and glass were placed in front of him, then sat back and took a piece of paper from his pocket. 'This message came through for you this mornin',' he said quietly. 'I figured it might be important.'

Bartell took the paper and ran his glance over it. His lips, almost hidden beneath the thick beard, twitched into a smile.

'Good news?' Bender enquired.

Bartell tossed down half of his drink before replying: 'You could say that,' he growled. 'Seems that nosy marshal I sent back on the train was shot while tryin' to escape from the Army. I guess I won't have to worry about him any more. He's been followin' my trail for some years.'

Bender's eyes narrowed slightly. 'You sure you can believe that? It could be a ruse to fool you.'

Bartell pursed his lips; then shook his head. 'My informant back in Coulson knows better than to give me the wrong information.'

'Then this calls for a celebration, my friend.' Bender raised his glass.

'Celebration?'

'To our continued partnership. You do intend to go on now that you still have someone who can keep you informed about these gold-shipments. I must confess that when you brought that man, Cleaver, back with you I thought that it would be an end to things.'

'I'll be the one who says if, or when, we go after more gold.' There was a note of underlying threat in the big man's tone. 'I don't intend to put my neck into a noose.'

'Of course not,' Bender replied hastily. 'I just meant that—'

'What you meant is that you want to get your hands on some o' that gold.' Bartell's voice was deliberately intimidating: 'Do you think I don't know there are a lot o' men who'd like to kill me if they get the chance. But they also know that with me dead, no one will find where it's hidden.'

Bender lapsed into an uneasy silence, then poured more whiskey into his glass. In spite of his position in the town, he knew better than to rile Bartell. He wanted that gold, all of it if possible. But what Bartell said was true. Dead, the outlaw was no use to Bender or anyone.

Bender allowed his glance to slide in the direction of the men standing along the bar. He knew that any one of them would kill Bartell without a second thought. Inwardly, he wondered if any of them had tried to follow the outlaw whenever they brought in any of the gold. It might be to his advantage to find out, he decided.

CHAPTER IV

SECRET MEETING

Sioux Falls looked deceptively quiet as Dave reined his mount on a small rise overlooking the main street a quarter of a mile away. On the surface, it seemed just like a dozen frontier towns he had known. But he knew that if one scratched the thin veneer of apparent peacefulness, there was a seething nest of violence underneath.

He allowed his gaze to rove along both sides of the street. There were plenty of townsfolk about and also men who wore guns low on their hips. As Carton had intimated, there was no law here except that which Bender dished out. Dave had come across such men before, men who had attained their positions by intimidation and murder.

To one side of the street stood the sheriff's office and further along he made out the tall building which he guessed was the Lost Trail saloon. He rolled a smoke and sat easily in the saddle, turning over in his mind the best way to approach this place. He reckoned that Bartell would have recognized him at that bridge during the hold-up. Now, there was also the added complication of this man Bender.

Whether Bartell already knew of his apparent death at the hands of the Army, he couldn't be certain. Furthermore, there was the possibility that Bender and the outlaw had already met and that the latter knew of the events of a few hours earlier. It was unlikely that Bartell would connect him with the man who had helped Carlton but it was a risk he didn't want to take.

Flicking the cigarette butt on to the hard earth, he turned his mount and rode a little way around the perimeter of the town, out of sight of anyone on the streets. Here there were numerous small alleys, most of them deserted.

Selecting one, he dismounted and led the stallion along it, keeping into the shadows. Somehow, he had to reach the Lost Trail saloon without being seen. Since it was quite possible that Bartell and his cronies would be in there at this time of day, he would have to work his way around to the back.

Already, even with that quick survey, he had the general lay-out of the place fixed firmly in his mind. Another alley angling away to his left led him deeper into the maze of squalid wooden buildings. He was almost halfway along it when a sudden movement brought him whirling round, drawing his Colt with a smooth, fluid motion.

The man stepped out of the shadows where Dave could see him. He was a small, grey-whiskered man who stood with his hands half-raised.

'Don't shoot, mister.' The cracked voice was little more than a whisper. 'If you're who I think you are, Miss Devlin sent me to watch out for you.'

Still holding the gun steady, knowing this could be a trap, Dave said: 'Who are you – and what do you know of Marie Devlin.'

The other gave a slight smile and slowly lowered his arms. 'The name's Wharton but most folk know me as Old Seth. Yours wouldn't be Stevens by any chance?'

'That's right.' Dave thrust the gun back into its holster. 'How did you know I'd be here?'

'Reckon Miss Devlin knows most o' what goes on in town,' replied the other hoarsely. 'Folk talk a lot in the saloon when they've had plenty to drink. I guessed you might come into Sioux Falls like this. Good thing too. Both Bartell and Bender are in the saloon right now.'

Turning, the old man gestured along the alley. 'Follow me. I'll take you to her.'

Still suspicious, Dave fell in beside the oldster, keeping a wary eye on his surroundings. The old man had certainly seemed to know his name and his story of watching out for him somehow rang true. Nevertheless, there still remained the possibility that he was being led into a trap.

Ahead of them, the alley intersected another and just as Dave made to step forward, the other threw out an arm to hold him back.

'Seems Bartell and Bender have some urgent business in mind,' Wharton whispered, nodding towards the far end of the alley. Edging forward a little way, Dave glanced along it. He made out the main street at the far end. As he watched a group of riders appeared. He instantly recognized Bartell's bulky figure, and behind the outlaw rode the man he had met that morning on Carlton's spread.

Wharton waited until they had vanished, then walked forward, stopping at the rear of the two-storey building Dave had noticed earlier. There was a small vacant area and jerking his thumb towards it, the old man said softly: 'You can leave your mount here. It'll be quite safe. Nobody uses this place.'

He took a key from his pocket, unlocked the rear door, swung it open, and motioned Dave inside. The place was clearly a storeroom with a flight of stairs at the far side. At the top was another door which Wharton opened slightly, peering through. Satisfied there was no one in sight, he said: 'Marie's room is the second along the corridor. She's expectin' you.'

From somewhere below came the sound of a tinny piano and loud voices. Making no sound, Dave walked to the second door and knocked softly. A moment later, the door opened and a woman stood there. She was almost as tall as himself. Long red hair fell in waves over her bare shoulders.

She wore a long red dress that matched her hair. Studying him closely for a moment, she asked; 'Are you the man Major Cauldwell told me about?'

Dave nodded. He felt inside his jacket pocket and brought out the star, holding it out in his palm. 'Dave Stevens. I'm a federal marshal but the major figured it wouldn't be wise to wear this while in Sioux Falls.'

'He was right.' Her voice was low and husky but her smile was hard. 'I'm glad Old Seth found you before any of the others.'

She stood on one side to allow him to enter and he smelled the perfume of her hair as he brushed past her. She closed the door and indicated the chair near the wall. Glancing around him, Dave guessed this was the dressing-room she used when working in the saloon.

There was a large dresser with various cosmetics on it and a large mirror at the back. Seating herself in front of the mirror, she said quietly: 'I suppose you know I work for the Pinkerton Agency, and the reason I'm here.'

Dave nodded. 'Evidently we're both here for the same thing – to get Bartell and his gang'

Her full lips curved into a smile. 'That will be more your job than mine. All I'm interested in is getting that gold back and seeing Bartell dead.'

'I heard about your brother from Cauldwell. I'm sorry it had to happen that way, betrayed by a coyote like Bartell.'

'Thanks. At least you now know why I volunteered for this job.' She picked up a brush and began brushing her long hair. 'You're sure no one knows you're here in town?'

'Quite sure. But I had a run-in with Jesse Bender this mornin'. He brought some of his men to try to run a rancher named Carlton off his spread. When they threatened to shoot the old man in the leg I had to step in.'

She turned that over in her mind for a moment,

then said: 'That could make things difficult. Bender has eyes and ears everywhere in this town.'

'You know much about him?' Noticing an ashtray on the dresser, Dave rolled a smoke and sat back, his legs stretched out straight in front of him.

'I work for him. This is his saloon like the three others.'

'And you're sure he doesn't suspect anything?'

Marie laughed softly. 'Bender is a fool where women are concerned. That's why the Agency decided to send me. A man riding in here would be suspected at once and I can get more information this way. Once those men down there are liquored up, they talk.'

'And what have you heard so far?'

She put down the brush and turned slightly to look directly at him. 'This may be nothing, or it may be important. One of Bartell's men joined them when they attacked that last train. A man called Cleaver.'

'I know him.' Dave said grimly. 'He was passin' along all of the information they needed.'

'It seems he's afraid of what the Army will do to him once he's caught.'

'They'll either hang him or shoot him.'

'Exactly and he doesn't intend to hang around too long to get his share of that gold. He wants to make it across the border into Mexico with his share. They were in the saloon last night but Bartell wasn't with them. He was trying to get some of the others to go with him the next time Bartell goes up into the hills.'

Dave stubbed out his cigarette and waited for her

to continue. Already, a plan was beginning to form in his mind. If Cleaver did go through with his scheme it might be possible to trail these men. It would be risky. These men would know all of the trails in this part of the territory but at the moment it was the only way of finding out where that gold had been concealed.

'You're thinking of following them, aren't you?'

'It seems the logical thing to do,' Dave admitted. 'You reckon you can keep your ears open and find out just when Bartell's likely to head out?'

'I'll do my best,' she promised. 'What do you intend doing now? It'll be dangerous for you if you're seen anywhere in town but you'll need some place to stay. It won't be safe for you to go back to Carlton's ranch. That'll be the first place they'll look for you if they should guess you've followed them here. You can stay the night here if you wish.'

'I don't want to put you to all that trouble,' Dave acknowledged. 'Furthermore, if anyone should find me here, you'd be in grave danger and either Bender or Bartlett might put two and two together. I figure my best chance is to camp outside o' town.'

Marie rose smoothly to her feet. 'There's an old shack about three miles north of here,' she said. 'It's been deserted for years. You should be safe there but you'll need some food and drink. Wait here and I'll bring some for you.'

She left the room, closing the door quietly behind her and leaving behind just a faint smell of perfume. While he waited, Dave turned over in his mind all she had told him. It was quite possible that some of

Bartell's men were now getting impatient with him, possibly no longer trusting him to share out the gold.

He knew it was doubtful if any of them would openly go against him. Bartell was a very dangerous man to cross. But if any should find where that gold was concealed, Bartell was a dead man. None of those gunslingers who rode with him would think twice about shooting him in the back.

The door opened a few minutes later and Marie came back carrying a parcel of food and a bottle of whiskey. 'This should last you until morning,' she said, handing them to him. 'If I need to get in touch with you at any time, I'll send Old Seth. Nobody will suspect him and he knows the territory around here like the back of his hand.'

'Thanks, Marie. Just watch yourself. We're dealin' with killers who'll shoot a woman down and think nothin' of it.'

'I'll be careful.' She opened the top drawer of the dresser and took out a derringer. 'I know how to use this as well as any man,' she said tautly. 'And if I have to use it, I will. You can be sure of that.'

Sheriff Mawson found himself sweating profusely as he sat uncomfortably in the saddle, riding ahead of the four men. He had hoped that Bender would send some of his own gunmen with him to force Carlton out, but Bender had refused point blank.

These men he had were the best he could get from among the townsfolk and he knew that none of them was either a gunman, or keen on the job in hand. Most of the citizens of Sioux Falls had had their fill of

Bender. Only the threat of his hired killers prevented them from running him out of town. Several times Mawson had wished he had the guts to throw his star back in Bender's face and tell him to get another man for the job.

But with this outlaw Bartell and his men back in town, that would be suicidal. This unholy alliance between the two had brought the town to where it was now: a powder-keg just waiting to explode.

Half an hour later, they came within sight of the small ranch house. Mawson cast a quick glance over the buildings and noted the large barn situated to one side of the house. Turning to the man on his left, he said harshly: 'You know what you've got to do, Clem? We'll keep Carlton talkin' while you fire those stables. With luck, the fire should spread to the house before they can get it under control.'

Clem nodded. He wheeled his mount and rode across the rough ground, keeping out of sight of anyone in the ranch house.

There was no one in view as the others rode into the courtyard, but a moment later two men emerged from the stables at one side. One Mawson recognized as Carlton. Both men held Winchesters in their hands.

'What do you want here, Sheriff?' Carlton called harshly. He kept his finger on the trigger, covering the five men. His companion moved a little to one side, ready for trouble.

Forcing himself to relax a little, Mawson replied: 'I got a complaint from Jesse Bender, Carlton. He claims two o' your men were on his spread last night and near on fifty of his steers are missin'.'

'Then Bender's a liar. None o' my hands have been off my spread for the past week. Bender came by this mornin' and tried to make me sell. He said nothin' about cattle bein' rustled then.'

'There's also a charge that you're harbourin' a wanted killer. One o' Bender's men was shot this mornin'. I want that man. Where is he?'

Carlton's lips twisted into a sneer. 'He ain't here, Mawson – and as far as I know, he's no killer.'

'Mebbe not, but that's for the law and the circuit judge to decide. Now are you comin' back to town with me, or do we have to—'

'You'll do nothin',' Carlton rasped. 'And if you're thinkin' of startin' anything, you'd better look behind you. There are two more rifles trained on you from that rise yonder.'

Mawson turned his head slowly. Out of the corner of his eye he had caught a glimpse of Clem edging around the corner of the stables. Had he not been concentrating on that, he might have heard the riders approaching.

Two men were seated in the saddle on a small knoll a hundred yards away. Both had rifles trained on him and his men. Swallowing thickly, he knew he had to keep Carlton talking for a little longer to give Clem a chance to get that fire started.

'Why won't you listen to reason, Ben?' he went on, forcing evenness into his voice. 'You'll have a fair trial, I promise you that.'

'A fair trial!' Carlton snorted derisively. 'A rigged jury made up o' Bender's friends. You're a fool if you reckon I'm goin' back into town with you, Mawson.' He raised the Winchester slightly, the barrel lined up on the sheriff's chest. 'Now get off my land before I pull this trigger.'

'You're not doin' yourself any favours, Carlton. I've got my duty to carry out. The next time I come, I'll have twenty men at my back. You can't buck the law.'

'The only law in these parts is Bender's – and you know it. Now move before I blow you out o' that saddle.'

'If that's the way you want it, Carlton, it's on your own head.' As he wheeled his mount, signalling to the men with him, he saw Clem move out of the shadowy interior of the stables and slip away into the trees on one side. There was a satisfied smile on Mawson's face as he rode away

Carlton watched them go; then turned back towards the house, halting sharply in his tracks as one of the men uttered a harsh cry. 'They've fired the stables, boss!'

Swiftly, Carlton called to the others. 'Get water!' he yelled urgently.

Without waiting to see if his command was being carried out, he began to run towards the stables. The fire had been started at the rear of the building and already it had taken a firm hold with flames licking up towards the roof. He pulled one of the horse-blankets from the nearby stall and began beating frenziedly at the fire.

Smoke was rapidly filling the air, getting into his throat and lungs. Behind him, Slim and Jeff ran in with buckets of water, throwing them on to the flames. Racking coughs sent spears of agony through Carlton's chest as he struggled to beat out the flames.

Fortunately, none of the horses had been stabled there at the time but it was soon evident that the fire was spreading furiously, out of control. The blanket was now on fire. He stamped on it, threw it behind him and reached for another as the men came back.

'It's hopeless,' Slim shouted, clutching at Carlton's arm and dragging him back. 'We'll never check it.' He began hauling the rancher away from the inferno. The side walls were now a mass of angry red.

'We've got to get out o' here,' Slim was yelling urgently at the top of his voice. 'The roof is goin' to fall in at any second.'

For almost a minute, with the heat blistering his hands and face, Carlton resisted, then allowed himself to be led outside. Through the tears that threatened to blind him, he gasped: 'Then we have to save the house. This wind will take the flames clear over to it. One o' you douse the house wall with water. We'll have to get this stable wall down before the fire spreads to it. If we can collapse it inward, we might have a chance.'

The next ten minutes saw a scene of frenzied activity. For a time, it seemed they were not going to succeed. Swinging a heavy axe, Carlton hacked at the base of the stable wall, attacking it with furious blows, putting all of his strength behind each swing. Chips of wood flew over his shoulders. Beside him, Jeff did likewise, attacking the stout wood as if it were one of Bender's men.

From inside the stables there came a tremendous crash. A vicious gout of flame spurted through the door as the burning roof gave way.

The choking smoke hampered their efforts but eventually the wall began to sway. Savagely, Carlton swung at it with the axe. With a crash, it fell inward, sending a shower of sparks high into the air. It still burned but now the fire was contained.

Slim came back and stood beside them, surveying the charred remains.

'How the hell did that start?' Jeff gasped.

Staggering back, Carlton sucked clean air into his lungs, wiping a streak of grime-stained sweat from his face. Only then was he able to speak, his voice little more than a hoarse croak. 'It was that goddamned sheriff. He had it all planned. He must've kept us talkin' while one of his men crept round the back. This is more o' Bender's doing.'

'At least we saved the house,' Slim muttered. 'But you can be sure Bender won't stop there.'

'You reckon I don't know that?' Carlton rasped hoarsely. 'I need more men: men who can handle a gun.'

'What about Stevens? You think he'd help you if we can get word to him?'

Carlton pondered that for a moment, then shook his head. 'Somehow, I've got a feelin' he's in town for somethin' more important than us. There was somethin' about him I couldn't quite figure out. But one thing I am sure about. He wants Bartell and he wants him bad.'

He went over to the pump and doused cold water

over his head, wiping the grime from his face. He knew his men were looking to him for answers, but at the moment he had none. Somehow, he doubted if the other small ranchers would help. Most of them were too scared of Bender, and the rest were like ostriches with their heads in the sand, believing that if they kept quiet, Bender wouldn't bother with them.

He wiped the back of his sleeve across his eyes. 'Ride into town, Slim,' he said at last. 'See if you can get word to Stevens.'

Slim rubbed his chin. 'How do I find him? If he's after Bartell, he won't want to show himself.'

'Have a word with Marie Devlin, the singer at the Lost Trail. If anyone knows where he is, I reckon she will. He was askin' about her this mornin'.'

Carlton waited until Slim had ridden off, then went into the house. Although he didn't want to admit it, even to himself, he now felt sure there was nothing he could do to prevent Bender from taking his ranch.

Following the directions Seth Wharton had given him, Dave made his way through a maze of alleys until he reached the northern outskirts of Sioux Falls. There seemed to be plenty of activity in the main street but he saw no one in the alleys.

Soon he came upon a narrow track which led away towards the wooded hills in the hazy distance. There was a pleasant warmth in the air and the sky overhead was clear and cloudless. Most of the way the track stretched across high ground, and he was able to scan the lower terrain for any other riders.

Several times he threw a quick glance over his shoulder, watchful for anyone who might be following him from town until eventually he was satisfied that he had not been seen leaving the Lost Trail saloon.

It was late afternoon when he reached the hills. Using the information Marie had given him, he soon found the narrow, winding track between two of the taller crests. Much of it was now thickly overgrown with brier and wildthorn and it was hard going for the mount.

Several times he was forced to dismount and lead the stallion through the denser parts. Quite clearly, he thought, this trail had not been used for years, had probably been forgotten by anyone in Sioux Falls.

By the time evening was drawing in, he was still pushing his way through a tangle of rough underbrush. Then, almost without warning, he came out into a wide clearing. In the centre stood the shack, a rough wooden structure but one which had obviously been well constructed.

There was little sign of decay in the timbers and he experienced a sudden sense of unease as he pushed open the door. It swung inward on noiseless hinges and a swift examination told him they had recently been oiled!

Smoothly, he drew the Colt from its holster and held it tightly in his right hand as he entered. In the dimness he made out a couple of chairs and a small table but little else. There was a small hearth midway along the opposite wall with a pile of grey ashes in the grate. He bent down and felt. They were cold, although he had the suspicion that there had been a fire there in the not too distant past.

Had Marie been misinformed? His sense of uneasiness increased as he went outside, scanning the trees all around the clearing. His first thought was that this might be the place where Bartell had hidden the gold but a meticulous examination of the ground and the interior of the cabin indicated no place where those large boxes could be concealed.

Not daring to light a fire, he settled himself in one of the chairs and ate a cold meal. Outside, darkness fell in earnest. He lit a cigarette and drew the smoke into his lungs; then started swiftly to his feet as he picked out a soft neigh from his mount.

Noiselessly, he crossed to the window. In the darkness, he could just make out the stallion and the nearest trees. Nothing moved in the shadows yet something had disturbed his mount and he knew from past experience not to ignore the warning.

There was the possibility it was a coyote or some other nocturnal animal but he intended to make certain. He drew the Colt and edged slowly towards the door, every sense alert.

He eased the door open and glanced out; then stepped away from the door. Everything was quiet. Nothing moved and he could see nothing in the shadows.

Then he stiffened abruptly as a voice called: 'Just hold it right there, mister. I've got a rifle trained on you. Now drop that gun.'

For a moment, Dave hesitated, trying to gauge where the man was. Then he let the gun fall, remaining absolutely still. It was a voice he did not recognize.

'That's better.' The dark figure emerged from among the trees ten yards away. As the voice had said, there was a Winchester in the man's hands and the fingers that held it were rock-steady.

As the man came forward, Dave saw that he was tall and broad-shouldered, possibly ten years older than he was, holding himself tautly erect.

'Just who are you, mister?' the other demanded. 'One o' Bartell's gunhawks?'

'No.' Dave decided to take a chance. 'I'm a federal marshal. Matter o' fact, I'm here after Bartell and his band.'

'That so?' There was a new note in the man's voice now, one more of curiosity than suspicions. 'I don't see a star on your shirt.'

'Do you think I'd be fool enough to show that around Sioux Falls? In that helltown, I'd be shot on sight. But it's in my jacket pocket.'

The rifle did not move an inch as the other said sharply, 'All right. Let me see it. And don't make any funny moves or they'll be your last.'

Slowly, Dave moved his hand, taking the star from his pocket. He held it out in the palm of his hand so that the other could see it. 'Satisfied?' he asked.

The man leaned forward a little, staring down at the badge. Then he nodded and lowered the rifle. 'I reckon you're who you say you are, mister. But what are you doin' here? How did you find this place?'

'Marie Devlin told me about it. She said it was a good place for me to hide out until I can make a move against Bartell.'

'Guess she was right about that.' The man motioned Dave to pick up his gun and go inside. 'I've been camped out here for some months now and you're the first man I've seen in this forest.'

He leaned the rifle against the wall near the door, then said: 'The name's Rick Thorpe. Like you, I'm here to kill Bartell.'

'You got something against him?' Dave asked, lowering himself into one of the chairs.

'Plenty. I was a lieutenant with the Confederates durin' the war. Three hundred o' my men were killed when the Yankees ambushed us. I managed to survive and when I found out that Bartell had sent word to the Yankees about our attack, I swore then that I'd hunt him down and kill him wherever he went. I owe it to those men who died because o' that traitor.'

'You're tellin' me you've been here for some months, yet you've never had a chance to get him?'

Thorpe shook his head. 'I guess you don't know Bartell like I do. He's damned cunning and clever. Never goes anywhere without those men of his except when he heads off somewhere to hide the gold they get. There's no one but him knows where it is. He plans everythin' down to the last detail. That's why no one's caught him yet.'

Thorpe went outside and returned five minutes later with an armful of wood and twigs which he began to place in the hearth.

'Aren't you afraid someone will find you here?' Dave enquired. 'That smoke can be seen for miles.'

Thorpe shook his head. 'Believe me, there's not a single livin' soul within five miles o' here. That's why I was surprised to find you. I spotted your mount outside.'

'How did you know it wasn't Bartell waitin' inside for you to show up?'

'Like I told you, he's as cunning as a desert rat. He'd never have left his horse in view. He'd have hidden it somewhere in the brush.'

Sitting back on his haunches in front of the blaze, Thorpe asked: 'Have you eaten lately?'

'Some which Marie gave me.'

'Guess you could find space for somethin' more. I've got a deer out there. I've been livin' off the land ever since I got here. I'll soon have somethin' cooked up.'

Half an hour later they were eating roast venison. When he had finished, Dave asked, 'Do you reckon that gold might be hidden somewhere in these hills, Rick?'

'Not a chance. I know all of this territory around here well enough to be sure that Bartell has never come here. He'll have chosen some place he knows, that he can find readily. Here, every tree looks the same as any other. My guess is it's somewhere to the south o' Sioux Falls.'

Thorpe paused, then went on: 'You got the makings of a smoke on you, Dave?'

'Sure.' Dave brought out his paper and tobacco and handed them to his companion.

Thorpe rolled the smoke, lit it and inhaled deeply. 'This is what I miss most. I seldom ride into town.' His lips quirked into a grimace. 'Strangers ain't welcome there as you've probably discovered for yourself.'

'And from what I've been told, Sheriff Mawson is in with Bender up to his neck.'

'That's true.' Thorpe nodded. 'I've had a run-in with Mawson myself when I first rode in. Bender offered me a job on his ranch. When I turned him down, Mawson came to see me; said my face and name were on a Wanted poster he had in his desk. But he made a big mistake.'

'Oh, what was that?'

'He came alone and tried to draw on me. I knocked the gun out of his hand and slugged him. There ain't no doubt it was Bender who put him up to it. But I have a few friends in town and get some provisions from them.'

'From the way talk goes around in that town, I'm surprised Bartell hasn't tried to hunt you down. He must know who you are and why you're here.'

Thorpe gave a quick grin. 'These woods are big. A man can hide here for years if he knows the right places.'

'And you know them all, I guess.'

Thorpe nodded. 'If Bartell did ride in here to flush me out, he'd be the one who'd get a bullet.'

There was a taut grimness to the other's tone which Dave noticed at once. Thorpe tossed the cigarette butt on to the earthen floor and ground it out under his heel. 'I'm turnin' in.' he said. 'I suggest you do the same. There's no cause to worry through the night.' He piled more brushwood onto the fire. 'We can talk again tomorrow. I have a feelin' we may be able to help each other.'

Dave brought his blanket and spread it out on the hard floor. He rolled himself into it and was soon asleep, the heat from the fire soaking into his bones. How long he slept before he was awakened by Thorpe shaking him by the shoulder it was impossible to tell.

Outside, it was still dark. Listening intently, Dave could hear nothing.

'What is it?' he asked in a low whisper.

'There's someone makin' his way along the trail. You must've been followed from town.'

Dave shook his head as he rose swiftly to his feet. 'I made damned sure I wasn't followed. You sure there's someone out there?'

'Hellfire, he's makin' so much noise pushing his way through the brush a deaf man could hear him a mile away.'

'Then it ain't anyone tryin' to sneak up on you,' Dave retorted. He paused as a fresh thought struck him. 'There's only one person it can be – Seth Wharton.'

'Old Seth? Why the hell should he come here?'

'You know him?'

'Sure. He's the swamper at the Lost Trail saloon.' Taking the rifle from the wall, Thorpe stepped silently outside with Dave close behind him. Now it was possible to pick out the sound of a rider picking his way through the trees only a short distance away.

A few moments later, the rider emerged into the clearing. A quiet, wheezing voice reached them. 'Is that you, Marshal?'

'It's me, Seth. Come on over.'

Wharton climbed stiffly from the saddle, paused as he caught sight of Thorpe, still holding his Winchester ready.

'You sure this man can be trusted?' There was a note of suspicion in Thorpe's harsh tone.

'Marie Devlin trusts him. She said she'd send him if there was any news about Bartell or Jesse Bender.'

'That's right, Marshal.' Still wary of Thorpe, the oldster approached. 'She sent me to tell you that Mawson tried to burn out Carlton this afternoon. Seems he kept Carlton talkin' while one o' his men fired the stable. It was just pure luck they managed to save the house.'

'You know what this means,' Thorpe muttered. 'From what I've heard, this *hombre* Bender doesn't have enough men at the moment to take on all o' the ranchers. My guess is that he's gone in with Bartell, probably hopin' to get his hands on some o' that gold.'

Dave turned that over in his mind. He knew that Bartell and those who rode with him were born killers. If Bender wanted them on his side, Bartell would want something in return. It wasn't like the man to bring in someone else to have a share in it. He had a feeling there was more to this situation than was showing on the surface.

Turning to Wharton, he asked: 'Is there anythin' more Marie asked you to tell me?'

Wharton nodded and wiped the back of his sleeve across his mouth. 'She overheard Bender and Bartell talkin' in the saloon this evening. Bender was sayin' there's word come through about another shipment.'

'Does she know when it's to be made?'

'No. But she reckons it could be soon.'

Dave rubbed the side of his face thoughtfully. Somehow, Bender was getting information from the Army post. If that were so, it confirmed his earlier suspicions that Cleaver had not been Bartell's only informer there. If Bartell was relying on Bender to get this information for him, it might explain why he was willing to aid the other against the ranchers.

'You're sure none o' these men suspect what Marie's doin'?' he asked. 'If they should figure out she's spyin' on 'em, they'll kill her, for sure.'

'I reckon she knows what she's doin'. It's no use tryin' to stop her. She's got a mind of her own and she won't change it for anyone.'

'No, I guess not,' Dave replied grudgingly.

'I'd better be gettin' back into town afore someone becomes suspicious,' Wharton said harshly. 'You ain't got any whiskey, have you? It gets mighty thirsty ridin' all this way.'

'I've got some,' Dave replied. He glanced across at Thorpe. 'It might be better if he was to stay here tonight, if you've no objections.'

'He can stay if he likes,' Thorpe replied.

Wharton shook his head. 'Thanks for the offer, mister, but there are eyes watchin' in town and if I was to wait until daylight they might start wonderin' where I've been all night. Under cover o' darkness, I can slip in and out without bein' seen.'

'Then take care, old-timer,' Dave said. 'Sooner or later, either Bartell or Bender is goin' to realize someone is passing information along to me. If that happens, both you and Marie Devlin could be in grave danger.'

CHAPTER V

ABDUCTION

Before dawn the next morning, Dave stood outside the shack, ready to move out. He had been turning things over in his mind during most of the night. Now he had made his decision. Thorpe stood in the doorway, watching him curiously. 'I guess you know you're takin' your life in your hands riding into town,' he said at last.

'Maybe.' Bending, Dave tightened the cinch under the stallion's belly. 'But the way I figure it, nobody in Sioux Falls knows who I am apart from Bartell and some of his men. If word has got through to him, he'll have been told I was shot tryin' to get away from the Army.

'I reckon it's now time to push both him and Bender. If they find out there's someone in town who's nosing into their affairs, one or the other might make a mistake. I've also got to find out if what Wharton told us last night about a further gold shipment being made is true.'

'If it is, and Bartell makes a play for it, you're surely not goin' to try to stop him alone.'

'That ain't part o' my plan,' Dave replied, swinging up into the saddle. Leaning forward, he went on: 'He's the only one who knows where it is and the only way I can find it is to get Bartell to lead me to it. Right now, he seems content just to leave it where it is and I can't wait for him to decide if or when he'll share it out with his men.'

'Could be he intends to take it all for himself,' opined Thorpe.

Dave shook his head. 'That won't be easy for him to do; not while the rest of his men are alive. They'd catch up with him before he got halfway to the border. Even in Mexico he wouldn't be safe. Sooner or later, they'd track him down and kill him.'

'So what's your plan?'

'First I aim to find out if there is another shipment being planned and, if possible, when and where. I don't doubt Bartell will go after it. This is an obsession with him. It has to be, otherwise he'd be satisfied with all he's got. Then I'm hopin' he gets away with it again, only this time I'll be waiting once he gets back to town.'

'And then you'll follow him?'

'It's the only chance I have. Whatever happens, I don't want Bartell dead until I've located it.'

'It sounds a mighty risky plan to me but I reckon you know what's best.'

'The first thing I intend to do is shake up that sheriff. He's the weak link in the chain. My guess is he'll talk just to save his own skin.'

'I hope you're right.' Thorpe hesitated, then said: 'There's only one thing I'd like to ask.'

'What's that?'

'If all o' this works out as you hope, I'd like to ride with you when you trail Bartell. I don't give a cuss about the gold. I just want to get that traitor in my rifle sights. I want to see him die for what he did durin' the war. Maybe that way, all those good men who died that day may rest in peace.'

Dave gave a brief nod. 'I guess I know how you feel. I'll think about it.'

Touching spurs to the stallion's flanks, Dave headed for the stand of trees, cutting down through the thick brush. He knew it was not going to be easy gaining the information he needed and, whatever happened, he didn't want to put Marie Devlin in any more danger than was necessary.

From his brief meeting with her, he knew she was a very determined woman and was probably capable of taking care of herself. But it would not be long before either Bartell or Bender began to suspect that he knew too much of what was happening. Bartell would immediately suspect one of his own men of loose talk somewhere in town and sooner or later would realize it was the saloon where such talk was likely to take place. Once he did, Marie would be in grave danger.

The sun had just risen when he came within sight of Sioux Falls. Already there were people about on the main street, with stores opening up for trade. He dismounted at the far end and tethered the stallion to the nearest hitching rail, then moved into the shadows. Some distance away, he recognized Mawson's portly figure. The sheriff was in deep conversation with Jesse Bender.

After a few moments Bender moved away into one of the narrow side streets. Dave waited for a few moments, then strode along the boardwalk to where the sheriff was staring moodily along the street. Mawson turned abruptly at his approach.

'I heard you had a little trouble with Carlton yesterday, Sheriff,' Dave said evenly. 'They reckon his stable mysteriously burned down just as you and your posse left. That seems a little more than coincidence to me.'

He saw the deep-red flush which immediately suffused the lawman's features and knew that his statement had hit home. Thinning back his lips, Mawson snarled: 'You seem to be takin' an unhealthy interest in what goes on around my town, stranger. If you're implyin' that I had anything to do with that, you'd better have some proof or you'll find yourself in jail.'

'I'm not implyin' anything, Sheriff. Just passing a remark.'

The other peered more closely at Dave, then said shortly; 'Somehow, I get the feelin' you're that *hombre* who shot one o' Jesse Bender's men out at the Carlton place a couple o' days ago.' His hand dropped towards the gun at his waist.

Lowering his voice so that he could not be overheard by anyone on the street, Dave hissed: 'Touch that gunbutt and you'll be a dead man before you draw.' He saw Mawson hesitate, then let his hand fall limply by his side.

'Just what is it you want with me, mister?' Mawson asked, swallowing hard. 'I ain't ever seen you before, yet you come ridin' into town, threatenin' me.'

'I'm just someone who doesn't like to see a man get an unfair shake o' the dice. It happens that Carlton is a friend o' mine and I don't aim to see him run off his ranch by a bunch a' killers.'

'If he goes against the law there ain't nothin' I can do but see that justice is done,' Mawson blustered.

Dave smiled, but there was no mirth in it. 'And who says he's committed a crime – you or Jesse Bender?'

'Now see here, I—'

'Don't try to deny it. You ain't the law here. Bender gives the orders and everyone jumps. I've seen it before in a dozen frontier towns. If you were a straight-shootin' lawman, that outlaw Bartell and his men wouldn't be walkin' around Sioux Falls, they'd be in jail waiting for the circuit judge to get here.'

Mawson tried to look Dave in the eye but failed miserably. His glance slid along the boardwalk to satisfy himself there was no one else within earshot. 'As far as I'm aware, Bartell ain't committed any crime in this town. Until he does, he and his men are free to come and go as they please.'

'So that's the way of it. And I suppose you've no knowledge o' the fact that Bartell's been told there's a further gold-shipment comin' by the railroad.'

Mawson stepped back a pace. He was suddenly

afraid of this man who seemed to know all that was happening. He took out a red handkerchief and mopped his forehead. 'You're loco, mister. I know nothin' about any gold.'

'You're lyin'. Both you and Bender are in with this outlaw up to your necks.' Leaning forward slightly, Dave thrust his face close up to the sheriff. 'If you want my advice, Sheriff, I'd turn in your badge right now and head out o' this town before everythin' explodes in your face. If Bartell should suspect that I got this information from you, I doubt if your life would be worth a plugged nickel.'

Struggling to summon up his composure in the face of this threat, Mawson blustered, 'You don't frighten me, whoever you are. If anyone should get out o' town, it's you. I can get a posse together and find you wherever you hide. Bartell and Bender are too big for one man to go up against.'

'We'll see about that. Now I suggest you walk back into your office and stay there.'

For a moment, Dave thought the sheriff meant to refuse. Then, turning abruptly on his heel, Mawson hurried away along the boardwalk. Smiling grimly to himself, Dave watched him thrust open the door and go inside. Evidently, he had judged Mawson correctly. Very soon, Bender would get to know what had happened.

Seated behind the table in his office, Mawson opened the bottom drawer and took out the bottle and a glass. His hand was shaking as he poured some of the whiskey into the glass, spilling it on to the top of the table. Gulping down half of the liquor, he tried to put his whirling thoughts into order.

Whoever this stranger was, he had certainly not been bluffing. How he had got this information was something he couldn't figure out. His first thought had been that the stranger was a federal marshal, but he had noticed no star on the man's shirt. Not that that was anything to go by.

He had just poured himself a second glass when the street door opened and Bender came in. One glance at the other's face told Mawson there was trouble.

Bender pulled out the other chair and lowered himself into it. 'I've just been talkin' with a couple o' my men,' Bender said harshly. 'It seems you didn't do a very good job out there at the Carlton place. His ranch house is still standing and that goddamned rancher has been ridin' around the other spreads, firin' 'em up.'

Bender made to go on, then noticed the whiskey bottle. 'You're startin' early,' he rasped. 'What the hell's got into you?'

'We're in trouble, big trouble,' Mawson muttered. 'It's that *hombre* who shot one o' your men in the hand.' The sheriff paused and took another couple of swallows.

When he didn't go on, Bender grated: 'All right, what about him?'

'He just came up to me in the street. He knows all about this gold-shipment Bartell mentioned.'

Bender's face hardened in disbelief. 'That's impossible. Only three of us know anythin' about that. Someone must've talked!'

'That's the way I'm thinking,' Mawson agreed. 'But who? Far as I'm aware, Bartell ain't told any of his men yet so it couldn't be one o' them and—'

'Well I ain't said a word,' Bender declared emphatically. The expression on his fleshy features changed abruptly. On the desk, his large hand clenched into a tight fist. 'That leaves only you.'

Wiping away the perspiration which beaded his forehead, Mawson stammered: 'I've never uttered a word about it, Jesse.'

'Then how the hell did this stranger know?'

'I've no idea.' Mawson knew he was in a tight spot, that his position was highly precarious. If either Bartell or the man facing him across the table should believe he was the one who had talked out of turn, they would have no compunction about killing him. He felt his mind racing as he struggled to come up with something.

He wiped his lips with the back of his sleeve and said tautly: 'There's one possibility we ain't considered. Have you ever discussed this shipment where you might have been overheard? There are eyes and ears all over this town and . . .'

He saw the other's eyes narrow and felt a faint wash of relief as he guessed Bender was considering that possibility. Then the other gave a ponderous nod. 'You may have somethin' there,' he agreed at last. 'We did mention it last night in the saloon. But there was no one near enough to overhear anything we said, except—' He broke off sharply.

'Except?' Mawson prompted.

He shook his head. 'No, it couldn't be . . .'

Mawson took out a second glass and slopped some of the whiskey into it. 'We've got to consider every possibility,' he said meaningfully. 'Was there someone?' He pushed the glass towards Bender.

Bender pursed his lips. 'Now I come to think of it, Marie was standing close beside the table. It's just possible she heard Bartell mention the gold. But she couldn't have told this *hombre.* I know for a fact that she's never left the saloon.'

He swallowed most of the drink and drummed with his fingers on the table.

'Then she must've somehow got word to him,' Mawson insisted. 'Nothin' else makes any sense.' He knew he was doing his utmost to persuade Bender that this was the answer, to divert any suspicion, rightly or wrongly, from himself.

'All right.' Bender agreed reluctantly. 'Perhaps it's time we had a little talk with Marie Devlin,' He took a thick cigar from his vest pocket, struck a match, and waved the flame over the end.

'Don't you reckon we should do that right away?' Mawson asked tensely. He half-rose to his feet, scraping back his chair.

Bender waved him back. 'There's no hurry. She ain't goin' anywhere. I'm sure that if she's the one, she doesn't suspect we know.'

'And this *hombre* who rode into town a couple o' days ago? What do we do about him? From what I saw of him, he could be mighty dangerous. He had the look of a gunfighter about him.'

'I'm quite sure Bartell will know how to deal with

him. He may be fast with a gun but he won't stand a chance against Ned's men.'

Finishing his drink, Mawson asked: 'What do you intend to do with that singer if she is the one givin' out this information. You ain't goin' to kill her?'

Bender was silent for several moments as if pondering the other's question, then he shrugged. Speaking through his teeth, he said: 'I don't like people who can't be trusted. I took her on in the saloon in good faith and if she's betrayed us, then she'll have to pay. For all we know, she could be workin' for the law.'

Mawson drew a hand down the side of his face as he sat back in his chair. 'Perhaps there's a better way o' dealin' with her,' he suggested hopefully.

Bender blew a cloud of smoke towards the ceiling. 'And what might that be?'

'Take her some place where she can't do any more harm, where we can keep her prisoner. That way, if she is in cahoots with this stranger and he gets wind of it, he'll come after her. It won't be difficult for word of her bein' kidnapped to be spread around town. Once he comes, we'll take care o' both of 'em.'

He sat back in his chair watching Bender closely. From the expression in the other's eyes, he knew that this idea appealed to him.

'You might have somethin' there,' Bender agreed. He stubbed out his cigar and got to his feet. There was a sardonic expression on his face as he added: 'Seein' that you're the law in town, Mawson, I reckon you'd better come along with me – just to make it all legal.'

Mawson reluctantly pushed back his chair and got up. He would rather Bender took Marie Devlin, but there was no point in arguing.

Together, they entered the Lost Trail saloon. Bartell was there, seated in the far corner. He glanced up sharply as they came in, then relaxed. As usual, the rest of his men were standing at the bar, talking and drinking.

Bender led the way to the table with the sheriff at his heels. Sitting down, he motioned Mawson to the other chair. Timidly, Mawson seated himself, his hands flat on the table. He felt hot and uncomfortable in the presence of these two men.

Bender signalled to the bartender and waited until the drinks had been brought and the 'tender had moved away, before speaking. 'It seems we've got trouble, Ned,' he said softly. 'Mawson and I have talked it over and think you'll agree we've come up with a solution.'

'Trouble?' Bartell raised his thick brows, a frown on his features. 'That's somethin' I don't like.'

Bender poured whiskey into his glass; then handed the bottle to the sheriff. 'It concerns that *hombre* I spoke about, the one who was at the Carlton ranch.'

'Well, what of him?' Bartell's close-set eyes bored into the two men.

'Somehow, he knows about this gold-shipment.'

Bartell's frown deepened into a scowl of anger. 'You sure about this?'

'He told me as much just a little while ago,' Mawson muttered.

'Then why the hell didn't you kill him – or at least throw him into jail where I'd have made sure he never got out again, alive?'

Mawson lifted his glass and took a couple of hasty swallows, wiping his chin where the liquor had spilled down it. 'He had the drop on me,' he stuttered. 'There was nothin' I could do.'

Bartell half-rose to his feet. 'Then someone must've talked.' His glance fell on the sheriff. Mawson shook his head vigorously. 'It wasn't me,' he protested. 'But we figure we know who it was.'

'We reckon that singer here must've overheard us talkin' about it last night,' Bender put in hastily. 'Somehow, she must've got word to this stranger.'

Bartell sank back into his chair. He nodded slowly. 'Then if you're right we have to get rid of her, permanently, before she can do any more talkin'.'

'I reckon we can get rid o' her and this *hombre* at the same time and with little trouble,' Bender put in smoothly. 'The sheriff and I are goin' up to her room right now. I know a little place just out o' town where we can keep her. If they're both in this together, it won't be long before this fellow goes lookin' for her and then we get 'em both.'

Staring down at his drink, Bartell considered that for almost a minute, a strange gleam in his eyes. 'I've been thinkin' about this stranger. We don't get many men ridin' into this town. Seems mighty odd he should just ride into Sioux Falls a few days after we held up that train.'

'You got some idea who he is?' Mawson queried.

Bartell nodded. 'Mebbe I've been given the wrong

information. If he's who I think he is, we're dealin' with a mighty dangerous and determined federal agent. His name's Stevens and he's been on my trail for years.'

'The man you were told had been shot escapin' from the Army?' Bender asked.

'The same.' Bartell pursed his lips into a grim line. His glance flicked from one man to the other. 'You're sure you can get this girl away and out o' town without bein' seen? Stevens could still be around and I don't want any mistakes.'

Bender finished his drink and got up. 'We'll take her out the back way. Just leave it to us, Ned.'

The two men went up the stairs without making a sound. Pausing outside the dressing-room door, Bender hesitated, then knocked softly. When a voice answered, he opened the door and went in. Behind him, Mawson threw a swift glance along the passage; then followed, closing the door behind him.

Marie Devlin was seated in front of the mirror. She turned as the two men entered. 'Is there something wrong, Jesse?' she asked.

'Why should there be anythin' wrong, Marie?' Even though Bender's tone was soft, there was a hint of menace to it.

'You don't normally bring the sheriff with you when you come here.' Marie turned, running her fingers over the various cosmetics in front of her.

'Well, right now, we're not sure, Marie,' Bender replied. He walked over to stand behind her, studying her through the mirror. 'Do you know a man named Stevens?'

Keeping her face completely emotionless, Marie said evenly. 'No, I've never heard that name before. Should I have?'

'That's what we want to find out.' Mawson spoke up from near the door. 'We have reason to believe this man is a federal marshal and someone in town has been passing information to him concerning Ned Bartell.'

With an effort, Marie forced herself to relax. She had no idea how much these men knew of Dave Stevens, but somehow they had discovered he was somewhere in town. She was aware that Seth had delivered her message to him up in the hills. Was it possible the old man had been followed?

She picked up the comb she began running it through her hair. Whatever happened, she had to keep her nerve. 'I don't know why you've come to me about this,' she said, forcing evenness into her voice. 'I just sing here. I know nothing about this man Stevens.'

'You're lyin'.' Bender spat the words at her. 'You were standing right next to our table last night when we were discussing things. You could have heard everythin' we said.'

'And assuming that I did, what concern is it of mine? I'm not interested in what you men talk about in the saloon.'

For a moment, Bender found himself believing her. Then logic asserted itself in his mind. He felt sure that Bartell had not yet told any of those men riding with him about the new shipment. He knew he hadn't talked to anyone. It had to be her.

'It's you all right.' he said roughly, keeping his voice low. 'No one else knew.'

'Then how do you think I could tell this man what you were talking about? I've never left the saloon.'

Lashing out, Bender caught her free wrist and hauled her roughly out of the chair. 'You sent someone to him with the message. But now you're finished. We've ways o' dealin' with people who can't keep their mouths shut. You won't be passing any more information.'

Before he could say anything further, Marie swung her hand. The steel comb caught Bender on the face, drawing a line of blood down his cheeks. With a sharp wrench, she managed to free herself from his grip. She dropped the comb and succeeded in pulling open the top drawer of the dresser. Her fingers closed around the derringer.

Bender reacted swiftly, cursing loudly. Before she had time to bring up the gun, his knotted fist struck her a savage blow on the side of the head, sending her crashing against the wall. The derringer dropped from her hand as she fell.

Bender took out his handkerchief and dabbed at the blood. Through his teeth, he snarled: 'I ought to kill the hellcat for that.' For a moment, his right hand dropped towards the Colt under his frock-coat. Then he thought better of it.

Bending, he caught her arms and pulled her unconscious form over his shoulders. To Mawson, he snapped: 'Check there's no one out there; then go down the back way in front of me.'

For a moment the sheriff hesitated. Then he

pulled himself together, recognizing the barely controlled anger in the other's tone. He opened the door slightly and peered out. The passage was empty. Voices reached him from downstairs but everything seemed normal. Slowly, he led the way down the back stairs and into the yard outside.

'Now go pick up my mount and bring it here,' Bender ordered. 'And make sure no one sees you.'

Mawson nodded. He slipped into the alley beside the saloon. He returned five minutes later, leading the mount. Bender swung Marie's unconscious form across the saddle and eased himself up. With a pull on the reins, he headed along the alley leading away from the main street. Mawson watched him go, then went back to his office.

Neither man had noticed the old man standing twenty yards away, completely concealed in the dark shadows.

CHAPTER VI

BAITED TRAP

Not wishing to be seen, knowing that now he had stirred up a hornet's nest in town, Dave located a small abandoned building near the outskirts. Gripping the bridle, he led the stallion inside. He doubted if any of the outlaws would recognize his mount, but a strange horse in Sioux Falls might attract some unwanted attention.

Leaning his shoulders against the wall, he took out paper and tobacco and rolled a cigarette. All he could do now was await any results from his talk with the sheriff. It would not take long before news of his presence got around. If he knew Bartell, all hell would be soon let loose until he was found.

Almost an hour passed and still there were no signs that any full-scale search had been launched. He was beginning to think that, for some reason, Mawson had not passed the word along that there was a stranger in town who seemed to know more than he should, when the stallion suddenly lifted its head, ears pricked forward.

Instinctively, Dave knew what that meant. The animal had detected a sudden sound. Swiftly, he drew his Colt. A moment later he picked out the shuffle of furtive footsteps in the alley. From the sound he guessed there was only one man, but there could well be others waiting at the other end of the alley.

He waited tensely until the man was almost level with the doorway, then stepped out, his finger hard on the trigger. He saw the other start back in sudden surprise.

'Don't shoot, Marshal. I've been lookin' all over town for you.'

Slowly, Dave lowered his gun. 'Has somethin' happened, Seth?'

Wharton gave a quick nod. 'It's Miss Devlin. I was watchin' the back o' the saloon when Bender and the sheriff came out. Bender had Marie slung over his shoulder. I guess he must've knocked her out.'

The old man paused and sucked in a deep breath.

'Go on,' Dave urged tautly.

'Bender sent Mawson for his mount and then headed out o' town with Miss Devlin over the saddle.'

Clenching his teeth, Dave muttered. 'I should have foreseen that somethin' like this might happen. They must have figured she was the one who gave me that information. Do you have any idea where Bender might have taken her?'

Seth shrugged his thin shoulders. 'If he's taken her somewhere out o' town there ain't many places where he could hide her. But since Mawson was with him, I guess he'd know.'

'That's true. But it ain't goin' to be easy getting Mawson on his own. He'll be on his guard now.'

Seth ran a hand across his whiskered chin. 'Mebbe if I was to turn you in? Bender's put out a reward for you, dead or alive.'

'Has he now! I wonder what trumped-up crime he's chargin' me with?' Dave turned the notion over in his mind. Somehow, he felt sure he could trust this old man. If they could reach the sheriff's office without being seen by Bartell or any of his gunmen, it might just be possible.

He reached a sudden decision. 'All right. Take my gun. We've got to make this look right.'

Taking the Colt, Seth said: 'Reckon you can leave your mount here. This place has been empty for years.'

Moving along the maze of narrow alleys, Seth led him towards the main street. Noise and the sound of a piano came from the nearby saloon but at this end of the street few people were around.

Seth thrust open the door of Mawson's office and pushed Dave inside with the gun in his back. The sheriff was seated behind the table, a half-empty bottle in front of him. His hand went towards his waist as he saw Dave.

'Relax, Sheriff,' Seth said hoarsely. He closed the door behind him.

A broad grin crossed the lawman's fleshy features as he noticed the gun. 'So you've come to claim the reward, Wharton.' He rose from his chair. 'As soon as

I have this *hombre* safely locked away I'll see that—'

'You'll see to nothin', Mawson,' Dave said thinly as Seth handed him the Colt. 'Now sit down and don't make any move towards your guns. You've probably guessed by now that I'm a federal marshal.' He took out his star and thrust it out in front of Mawson. 'I'd be perfectly within my rights to lock you in your own cells and call the circuit judge.'

'Federal marshal or not, you've got no jurisdiction in Sioux Falls. I'm the elected law here and I—'

Dave smiled but it was not a pleasant grin. 'I've got enough evidence to hang you and your cronies, and you know it.'

The flush on the lawman's face faded swiftly to be replaced by an ashen look. Somehow, he managed to bluster: 'So you'll lock me up. Believe me, Stevens, I'll be out o' jail before sundown once Jesse Bender hears o' this. Then it'll be you we'll string up.'

Straightening up, Dave said tautly: 'Knowin' how this helltown is run, I don't doubt that. But speakin' of Bender, where is he now? Where has he taken Marie Devlin?'

Mawson's scared glanced flicked from Dave to Wharton. He ran his tongue across lips gone suddenly dry. 'How should I know where Bender is or who he's got with him?'

'You know damned well because I saw you both take her out o' the saloon,' Seth butted in.

For a moment, Mawson stared at the whiskey bottle on the table. His hand reached out for it, then he drew it back. 'All right, all right. I'll tell you. But it won't do you any good. You'll never find her. It's some place in the hills to the east. That's all I know.'

Keeping the Colt levelled on the sheriff, Dave grated: 'You'd better be tellin' the truth, or the next time you see me, will be your last. I have a particular dislike o' crooked lawmen. Now – get on your feet and leave your guns on the table.'

Reluctantly, the other rose from the chair. For a moment, the thought of action entered his mind, then one look at the expression on the features of the man who faced him, made him change his mind. Slowly, he took out the guns and laid them on the table.

'Now get inside one o' those cells.' Prodding the sheriff hard in the back, Dave forced him across the room and into the short passage at the rear, taking down the bunch of keys from the wall as he passed.

Once Mawson was inside the cell Dave reversed his gun and struck the sheriff a hard blow on the back of his head. 'We don't want him yellin' to anyone who might come in,' he said grimly, heaving the inert body on to the iron bed.

He locked the cell door and went back into the office. 'I'd hoped we'd get more information from Mawson,' he said sombrely. 'Whether he really knows anythin' more, it's hard to say.'

'So what do we do now?' Seth asked.

'We?' Dave raised his brows. 'I intend to ride up into those hills and try to find Marie before Bender decides to kill her. She's a hard woman but if that killer applies any pressure, she might talk. I want you to stay out o' this. You've already done a lot and I'm mighty grateful, but—'

'You won't have a chance o' finding where Bender's taken her unless you take me along with you,' Seth declared emphatically. 'I know those hills better'n anybody in this town. Did some prospectin' up there years ago. Bender ain't goin' to keep her in the open. That would be too dangerous. My guess is he's headed for the mine-workings. It's the best place for him to keep her. Nobody's been up there for more years than I can remember.'

Tightening his lips into a hard line, Dave replied: 'I appreciate your help, old-timer. But my guess is that this is just what Bender is hopin' for. He knows I'll get word o' what's happened and go after her. He'll be up there waitin' for me.'

'I can still ride and handle a gun,' Seth declared defiantly. 'He won't be expectin' me.'

Dave nodded reluctantly. 'All right. Get your horse and gun and meet me where you found me.'

After throwing a swift glance along the street, Dave slipped out of the office and away from the main street. He didn't like the idea of taking the old man with him. It meant he would have to keep an eye on him while watching out for Bender, but there was some logic in what Seth had said.

When Marie recovered consciousness she was lying on something hard and rough. With an effort, she opened her eyes and turned her head slowly, struggling to take in her surroundings. Her jaw ached and there was a bruise along the side of her face.

There was the bright glow of a fire at the edge of her vision. By the light of the dancing flames she made out rocks and huge, misshapen boulders surrounding a clear space. There was a faint glow of daylight but it was far away and she guessed she was at the end of a long tunnel.

She tried to move her arms to push herself up into a sitting position only to discover that her hands were tied in front of her. Glancing down, she saw that a rope bound her ankles together. Little fragments of memory returned. She recalled Bender and the sheriff coming into her dressing-room and accusing her of passing information to the federal marshal, of trying to reach the derringer in her drawer and Bender's bunched fist lashing at her before she could use it. After that, there was nothing.

A sudden sound, accompanied by a movement, drew her attention towards the far end of a tunnel. In the glow from the fire, she made out the tall, thin figure advancing towards her.

A moment later, Bender stood by the fire, looking down at her. 'So you're awake at last,' he said harshly. He shook his head. 'It really is a pity it has to end this way. I'd taken quite a fancy to you. I trusted you completely.'

He squatted down on his heels a few feet away. 'I never had you figured as workin' with the law. What made you decide to throw in with this lawman?'

Marie ran her tongue around the inside of her mouth. The pain in her jaw made it difficult to speak. 'I've already told you,' she mumbled. 'I don't know this man you're talkin' about. I've never even met him.'

'But you've managed to get word to him and I

think I know who acted as your messenger – that old fool Seth Wharton. He was always hanging around your dressing-room.' The smile on his face broadened. 'You reckon he won't talk once we bring him in? A couple o' Bartell's men were friends with the Apache and learned some tricks from them. They'll soon get the truth out o' him.'

Marie felt a finger of ice brush along her spine. She knew this man meant every word he said. He worshipped only gold and the power it brought. He would kill anyone who got in his way and not give it a second thought.

'You won't get away with this. Sooner or later this stranger will get you.'

Bender straightened up with an effort. 'Ah, but there you're wrong. I've seen to it that he knows I've got you and it won't take him long to come after you. But one o' my men is lyin' in wait outside.' Leaning forward, he said thinly: 'You see, I've thought of everythin'.'

'And how long do you intend to keep me here?' Somehow, Marie kept the tremor out of her voice.

'Just until this nosy marshal turns up and we're rid of him for good.'

'And then what? You mean to kill me too?'

Bender considered that for a moment, then shook his head. 'I reckon that once this lawman is out o' the way, you can't do us any more harm. I can see to it that you stay in Sioux Falls. But I guess that will depend on Bartell. He has no likin' for people who open their mouths too much.'

Marie felt a little shiver pass through her at these

words. Since working for the Pinkerton Agency, she had come across men such as these before. To them, human life was cheap. She doubted if Bartell would allow her to live. He had far too much at stake to afford taking any risks.

For a moment, Bender stood with his hands on his hips, staring down at her. Then, apparently satisfied she was helpless, he moved away. Straining forward, she saw he was heading for the tunnel mouth.

She watched him as he disappeared around the edge of the tunnel. She sucked in a deep breath and tthrust herself hard against the rock, pushing herself into a sitting position. If she could reach the fire, she thought desperately, there was a chance she might burn the rope around her wrists.

At that moment, she didn't pause to consider what she could do if she succeeded in freeing herself. All she knew was that, somehow, she had to get free. Somehow, she had to warn Dave. With an effort, she managed to turn. Drawing up her knees, she heaved herself away from the rock. Working her legs, she slowly eased herself across the rough floor, ignoring the pain as jagged stones cut into the lower part of her back. Several times she had to pause to gather her strength for a further effort.

Twisting her head, she saw the burning branch which lay barely a foot from her. Gingerly, she eased herself forward. The heat from the fire burned her face. Gritting her teeth, she moved her hands towards the branch an inch at a time.

It took all of her control not to scream aloud as the flames licked at her hands. Summoning all her resolve, she held out her hands as the flames caught at the stout rope. Several times, she had to pull back as her flesh began to burn. Slowly, the flames took hold.

She pressed her lips tightly together, afraid that at any moment Bender would return. Somehow she bore the pain. Pulling back, she exerted all of her strength, forcing her hands apart. Then, with a sudden snap, the rope parted. Sucking the hot air into her lungs, she leaned forward, tugging at her bound ankles.

The cord around her legs had been tied tightly and, in spite of the taut control she had over her actions, her fingers were trembling. Gradually, the knot loosened. Five minutes later, she was standing, swaying slightly with the exertion. Leaning momentarily against the wall of the tunnel she fought down the dizziness which passed through her.

She knew her position was precarious in the extreme, that even if she managed to evade Bender, she was still several miles from Sioux Falls. There was also that other man whom Bender had said was somewhere outside, keeping watch in case Dave came to her rescue. Perhaps if she managed to conceal herself somewhere among the rocks, she might have a chance to warn Dave of his danger.

Slowly, she approached the entrance of the tunnel. Pressing herself tightly against the rocks, she risked a quick glance. Bender was still nowhere in sight but she doubted if he would have gone far, even though believing she was securely tied up.

The ground in front of the tunnel was flat and

open and she knew she could not risk running across it to reach the tall boulders on the far side. To her left was a sheer wall of smooth stone, impossible to climb. On her right, however, some ten yards away, was a huge pile of rocks where it might be possible to hide.

Holding up the hem of her dress, she gathered herself and then began to run towards the rocks. She had almost reached them when the shot rang out from the opposite side of the clearing. The bullet scored a small furrow in the stone less than a foot from her.

She fell against the rock, then stood there, unable to move. Bender walked slowly towards her, the Colt held firmly in his right hand. There was a leering smile on his face as he said harshly: 'You're a mite too tricky for your own good, Marie. Maybe I should kill you after all. Guess it won't make any difference to this *hombre* when he does come lookin' for you. He sure won't be ridin' back to town.'

'Then why don't you shoot me?' Marie uttered the words through tightly clenched teeth 'That's what you intend to do anyway. I know far too much about you and your dealings with Bartell. Could be that if the townsfolk know you for what you are, a woman-killer, you won't last long in town either.'

For a moment, a spark of fury showed in Bender's close-set eyes. His teeth showing in a savage grin, he lifted his hand. Marie flinched, expecting him to pull the trigger of the Colt. Instead, his other hand came round hard. It was not a punch as before, but the resounding slap across the side of her face threw her against the rock.

She felt her knees give but, with a conscious effort of will, she managed to remain upright.

Still smiling, he stepped back a couple of paces. 'No, I don't intend to kill you – yet. I want you alive to see this *hombre*'s body lyin' on the ground. Now get back inside the tunnel. This time, I'll make sure you don't try to get away.'

CHAPTER VII

DANGER TRAIL

With Seth leading the way, the two men headed swiftly away from Sioux Falls towards the hills which showed as a dark blur along the horizon. Much of the country here was barren, covered only with mesquite and other stunted bushes which managed to extricate a precarious existence from the soil.

It was only towards the south and east that the richer pasture land began. From what he had heard, most of that belonged to Jesse Bender. Sitting taut in the saddle, his keen gaze watching the surrounding terrain, he followed Old Seth's uncompromising back.

There was the possibility that Bender might be watching this region, but somehow he doubted it. If the rancher had taken Marie into some old gold-workings, he would need to keep a constant watch on her. There was little doubt she would try to make her escape if the slightest chance presented itself.

Edging his mount forward, he came up alongside Wharton. 'Just where are these workings, Seth?' he asked.

Lifting his right hand, Wharton pointed towards a spot a little way to the left. 'The old track is still there. It ain't easy to negotiate now. Like I said, it must be close on thirty years since those seams ran out.'

'And how long is it since you were here?'

Seth pursed his lips, then shrugged. 'Fifteen years ago, I reckon. I sort o' figured there might still be a little left. I stayed up here for nigh on three weeks but never found any.'

It took them almost an hour to reach the hills where they rose high and gaunt in the light of the westering sun. Here there was a multitude of dark shadows where a man with a gun might conceal himself.

'We'll have to move carefully now,' Wharton said thinly. 'My guess is that Bender wants you to come after him for the girl. If so, he could've laid a trap. There's also another problem. We can only take the horses so far. The rest o' the way we have to go on foot.'

Dave gave a brusque nod. 'Then lead the way, old-timer. I guess you know these hills better'n I do.' He threw a quick glance towards the trees. 'How far is it to this place?'

'Close on a couple o' miles,' replied Wharton. 'The track is a little further on. Once we reach it, make as little noise as possible and keep your eyes and ears open. It's too quiet for my liking.'

The track, when they reached it five minutes later,

was little more than two feet wide. Stiff branches formed a cover over it and they were forced to ride with their heads low over their mounts' necks. Around them, the only sound was the soft scrape of hoofs on the hard earth.

He had expected to find these hills full of wildlife. Curiously there was none. As Seth had said, the place was unnaturally quiet, looming around them, filled with a deathlike silence. If they were on the right track, Bender had certainly picked the right spot to take Marie.

In front of them, the trail began to ascend steeply and the horses were finding it difficult to keep their footing. They progressed in this way for more than a mile before Seth raised his right hand to call a halt. 'We'll tether our mounts among the trees,' he said softly. 'Soon we'll come out among the rocks and that's where there's like to be trouble.'

Dave stepped down from the saddle, eased his Winchester from the scabbard and then led his mount a little way among the trees. He looped the reins around an overhanging bough. The stallion had been well trained and there was no chance of it straying.

A little way further on the trees thinned out and the two men came out into the open. Ahead of them, the track still continued towards a low crest which stretched, seemingly endlessly, to left and right. Keeping his head well down, Seth scrambled towards it, motioning to Dave to do likewise.

Lying on his stomach close beside Dave, Seth murmured softly: 'The ground now levels off for a piece and then drops pretty steeply towards the old workings. My guess is that if Bender has brought her here, he'll be inside the tunnel waitin' for you. This ain't goin' to be easy. He'll be able to stay under cover and there's a wide open space you'll have to cross to get to him. He can pick you off before you cover half the distance.'

Dave raised his head slowly until his eyes were just above the rim of rock. He scanned the terrain in front of him. Slowly, he allowed his gaze to take in everything.

'See anythin'?' Seth asked..

'Nothin'. Could be you're right and Bender is waitin' inside the tunnel. Reckon I—'

He broke off sharply as a faint sound reached him. It had been some distance away but in the clinging stillness it had sounded abnormally loud. It was also a sound he instantly recognized. The scrape of a match.

Narrowing down his eyes, he made out the faint cloud of tobacco smoke a moment later. 'Bender's not takin' any chances,' he murmured softly, placing his lips close to Seth's ear. 'He's got a man among those boulders yonder. Seems he doesn't suspect we're here. He's just built himself a smoke.'

Seth twisted his lips into a grimace; then jerked his thumb towards their left. A moment later he had disappeared around a large rock formation, moving as silently as a cat.

Dave guessed the old man's intention. While Seth caused a distraction, it would give Dave a chance to get a bead on the dry-gulcher. Moving slowly, Dave worked his way to the right, away from the trail. Now that he knew where the man was concealed, he would be ready for any move the killer made.

He eased his shoulders against the rough stone, checked the Winchester, then waited. He did not have long to wait. A sudden loud rattle sounded in the near distance as several large stones bounced down the slope.

Dave saw the shadow a second before he saw the man as the other shifted his position. The man was leaning forward against a boulder, his rifle trained on the spot where Wharton was concealed. Swiftly, Dave thrust himself upright, his finger as straight as a bar across the trigger.

'Drop that rifle, friend,' he said softly, a note of menace in his voice, 'or I'll let you have it in the back.'

He saw the man stiffen abruptly. For a moment, Dave thought the other meant to whirl and bring the weapon to bear on him. Then, slowly, the man reached out his arm and let the rifle fall among the rocks.

'Now you're showin' some sense. Just shuck that gunbelt. Don't try anythin' or it'll be the last thing you ever do.' He saw the man reach forward, his hands close to his Colts. Then, as if realizing he didn't stand a chance of drawing the Colts from leather, he unbuckled the belt and tossed it away behind him.

Dave lowered himself cautiously down the slope until he was standing a couple of feet from the other. 'Now turn around and keep your hands where I can see 'em.'

The man turned slowly. He was tall, black-bearded. There was a jagged scar along one cheek which gave a permanent twist to his mouth. His eyes, deep-set beneath thick brows, glared at Dave.

Moments later, Wharton appeared. 'He's one o' Jesse Bender's men,' he said without any hesitation. 'His name's Cranton. I've seen him around town with the others.'

'I didn't doubt it for one minute,' Dave replied. 'It seems he ain't very good as a look-out.' He stared straight into Cranton's eyes. 'Are there any more o' you hiding among these rocks?'

Cranton's lips twisted even further as he snarled: 'Right now there are three rifles trained on you and your friend. You ain't goin' to get anywhere near Jesse and you'll be dead before he starts on the woman.'

Dave saw Seth cast an apprehensive glance around. Watching Cranton's eyes, Dave knew immediately that he was bluffing.

'There ain't anyone else around,' he said confidently. 'If there were, we'd be dead by now.' Stepping forward, he prodded the other hard in the chest with the barrel of the Winchester. 'If you want to get out o' this alive, I suggest you start talkin'. Bender's somewhere around and my guess is he's in the tunnel getting' ready to kill Marie if I should put in an appearance.'

'Reckon you'd better go along and see,' muttered the other, trying to force defiance into his tone.

Dave hesitated for a moment, then nodded. 'Guess I'll do just that. You reckon you can keep an eye on this *hombre*, Seth?'

Wharton grinned. 'He won't give me any trouble.'

Dave stepped back and began to descend the pitted surface of the rocks. Down below, he made out the wide open space. It looked deserted but he knew that could be an illusion. Bender was well aware that he was coming – and he was no fool.

Even with Cranton posted as look-out, he would not feel completely secure. Sliding the last three feet among sharp-edged rocks, Dave reached the bottom and crouched down. The tunnel mouth was an irregular black opening in the rock wall some thirty yards away. He could see no movement but there was a faint, flickering yellow glow just visible deep inside.

If he tried to make it across, he would be a perfect target for anyone just within the entrance. To his right, the bare side of the hill rose vertically for more than a hundred feet. On the other side, however, the level ground narrowed and, from the lie of the land, he judged he would be out of sight of anyone inside the tunnel.

Knowing it was his only chance, he moved away to his left, keeping his head well down. It took him the best part of ten minutes to circle around the perimeter. Crouching down on the far side of the open area, he waited tensely. There was still no sign of activity around the tunnel mouth and he guessed Bender was inside, keeping a close watch on Marie.

For a moment he debated his best plan of action. Then he laid the Winchester against the rock and withdrew his Colt, checking the chambers carefully. The rifle was useful for long-range shooting but at close quarters the revolver was the ideal weapon.

Very slowly, he edged towards the dark, irregular opening, making as little noise as possible. A moment later he halted abruptly as the unmistakable sound of footsteps reached him.

Bender's harsh voice came from just inside the tunnel. 'Everythin' all right out there, Cranton? Any sign o' this marshal?'

When there was no reply, Bender called again, this time more loudly and urgently. 'What the hell are you doin', Cranton?'

By now, Dave had judged Bender's position to within a few inches. The man was standing against the far side of the tunnel less than twelve feet away. Tensing himself, Dave stepped away from the rock, caught a glimpse of Bender, and raised the Colt. He squeezed the trigger twice.

Both bullets missed as the other flung himself back into the shadowy interior. The next instant there came the vicious hum of a slug past Dave's face as Bender recovered himself.

'So you've finally shown up, lawman.' There was both surprise and fury in the other's tone. 'I don't know how you got past Cranton but you'll never get me or the woman. Make one move I don't like and she gets a bullet in the head. You got that, Marshal?'

'You're finished, Bender,' Dave called back. 'Better let Marie go and give yourself up or you'll never get out o' there alive.'

'No?' There was a taunting quality to the other's tone now. After a short pause, Bender called: 'Marie! Come over here. Slowly now, or I'll kill you.'

Dave guessed that Bender was trying to rile him into some rash action. With an effort, he forced himself to think coolly and calmly. He knew Bender meant every word, that he would shoot Marie in cold blood if she didn't do exactly as he said.

The soft sound of someone shuffling across the hard ground inside the tunnel reached him a moment later and he knew that Marie had moved forward and was now standing close to Bender, whose gun would be trained on her.

A split second later, a shot rang out. Dave flinched, believing that Bender had carried out his threat. Then he realized it had been a rifle shot. From the corner of his vision he noticed Seth standing among the rocks thirty yards away. Scarcely had the whine of the ricochet died away from where the old-timer had deliberately aimed to one side of the tunnel mouth before he ran forward.

Bender was standing with his back against the tunnel wall. He held his Colt in his right hand. His other arm was locked tightly around Marie's neck.

'Drop that gun you're holdin',' Bender snarled. 'And tell your friend over there to do the same with the rifle. If you don't, your girlfriend gets the next bullet through her pretty head.'

Still gripping his Colt, Dave shouted: 'Do as he says, Seth. Drop your rifle.'

He heard the brief clatter as Seth released his hold on the Winchester. As though waiting for this slight distraction, Marie made her move. With a savage wrench, she bent her head forward and dug her teeth into Bender's wrist.

Uttering a sharp cry of agony, Bender pulled his arm away and in the same moment, Marie dropped to her knees. Dave did not hesitate. Jerking up the Colt, he loosed off a single shot.

For a moment, Bender remained upright, struggling to force life into his arm and lift his own gun. Then his eyes rolled up in his head and he fell forward across Marie. Dave ran into the tunnel and helped her to her feet.

'Are you all right, Marie?' he asked anxiously.

She nodded, dusting the dirt from her skirt. 'I'm fine. I knew you'd come but when Bender said he had a man waiting in the rocks, I tried to warn you.'

'Luckily, he didn't reckon on Seth coming with me.' Glancing up, he saw the other approaching. 'What happened to Cranton?'

Seth grinned. 'He's still up yonder. I figured you might need a little help here so I hit him over the head.' He glanced down at the body just inside the tunnel. Rubbing a hand down his cheek, he muttered: 'I guess you know that once this gets around town, there'll be hell to pay.'

'You mean from Bartell?'

'Not just him. Bender had a lot o' men with him. Some might just ride on over the hill when they hear he's dead but I reckon most of 'em might side with Bartell.'

Dave pondered that for a moment, then shook his head. 'My guess is that Bartell is goin' to be mighty pleased that Bender is dead. Not that he'll shout it, of course. But the way I see it, Bender was after some o' that gold. Now there's one less to share it.'

Turning back to Marie, he said: 'Now we have to decide what to do with you. It's certain you can't go back to the Lost Trail saloon. That would be far too dangerous. Bartell wants you silenced.'

'So where can I go? I don't intend to leave Sioux Falls until I've finished the job that was assigned to me.'

'There's that shack where I spent the night. Trouble is, it ain't as empty as you thought.'

Seth butted in before Dave could explain.'Some *hombre* by the name o' Rick Thorpe has taken it over.'

A puzzled frown creased Marie's forehead at the mention of this name. 'I've heard that name before. My brother sometimes mentioned a Lieutenant Thorpe.'

'Then he must be the same man. He told me he was a lieutenant in the Confederate Army. Like us, he means to kill Bartell for sellin' those military secrets to the North. It seems he lost some two thousand men when he led them into that ambush.'

'What do we do with him?' Seth asked, gesturing towards the body near the wall.

Pressing his lips into a tight line, Dave hesitated, then said: 'We'll leave him here and get the sheriff to send someone out for him. As for that gunhawk back there, we'll take him with us.'

Seth frowned. 'If you're figurin' on Mawson tossing him into jail to await trial, you're headin' along the wrong trail there, Marshal. Even if Bartell is content to let him rot there, the sheriff will let him go. Cranton has too much on Mawson to allow him to stick around until the circuit judge gets here.'

'Maybe you're right,' Dave conceded, 'but there's little else we can do at the moment. Right now, we'd better get Marie into a safe place. Bender's bronc should be around here someplace. We'll take Cranton in across his own saddle. Then I'll need you, Seth, and Thorpe, to keep a constant watch on Bartell. The minute he rides out with his gang, they'll be headin' for that next gold consignment and I want to know about it.'

CHAPTER VIII

DESPERATE MEASURES

Leaving Wharton to take Marie back to the shack in the hills, Dave swung off the trail back to Sioux Falls. Beside him, Cranton sat slumped in the saddle, barely conscious, his hands tied securely to the pommel

As they came within sight of the town, Cranton lifted his head and muttered thickly: 'You'll never get away with this, Stevens. Once they hear that Jesse is dead, all o' the others will hunt you down and I'll be out o' jail before nightfall.' His twisted lips formed into a leering grin. 'As for this woman you're obviously sweet on, Bartell will finish her.'

Dave swung on him. 'Just keep your mouth shut, Cranton, or you might not reach town alive.'

'That's just what you'd like, ain't it? Shoot me here

so there's no one to testify you shot down Jesse in cold blood.'

With an effort, Dave controlled the surge of anger in him. 'No one in town is goin' to believe that except Bartell and that crooked lawman you've got as sheriff,' he retorted. 'I reckon you'd better look to your own hide because the next time we meet, I'll kill you.' The veiled threat in his tone silenced the other.

As they rode into the main street, Dave noticed the curious glances he got from the folk on the board-walks. It was clear everyone knew that his prisoner was one of Bender's hirelings and they were probably wondering what had happened to Bender himself. He came to a halt in front of Mawson's office, where he dismounted and ordered Cranton down.

He drew his Colt and rammed it hard into Cranton's back, thrusting him through the door. The sheriff was seated behind the desk, a sheaf of papers in front of him. He looked up sharply as they entered, his gaze switching from Dave to Cranton, marking the dried blood on the side of the gunhawk's head.

Thrusting the chair back, Mawson got to his feet. 'What the hell is this?' he demanded. 'This man works for Jesse Bender. He—'

'I know who he is,' Dave snapped harshly. 'Just as you'd planned, I followed Bender's trail to where he was holdin' Marie Devlin prisoner. Bender's dead and this coyote made the mistake o' trying to bush-whack me. Reckon you'd better put him into one o' your cells.'

'He's lyin', Sheriff.' Cranton spat the words out

through his teeth. 'He shot Jesse without givin' him a chance to draw his gun.'

'Well now, that puts a different face on things.' Mawson pulled himself up to his full height. 'It's Cranton's word against yours, I guess. I know who the folk in this town will believe, given the choice between that of a well-known citizen and that of a stranger who rides in intent on stirrin' up trouble.'

'Then perhaps this will get them to change their minds.' Dave took the star from his pocket and placed it on the desk.

Mawson and Cranton stared down at it as if mesmerized. Eventually, the sheriff regained some of his bluster. 'I told you, you've got no jurisdiction in this town and as long as I'm the law, I—'

'You'll do exactly as I say.' Dave's voice was like an iron bar. 'Otherwise, I pass word along to the Army that you're harbourin' the outlaws who've been holdin' up their trains and killin' their men. Before you know it, this town will be overrun by soldiers and it could be they'll also uncover certain things about you that you'd rather didn't come out into the open.'

He saw Mawson's face blanch and knew the threat had hit home. Swallowing thickly, noticing the gun still in Dave's hand, Mawson said haltingly: 'Very well, I'll lock him in one o' the cells. But this ain't the end of it. Once Bartell gets word o' this, he'll have him out o' jail by mornin'. Even if the Army does come, you won't be alive to meet 'em.'

'I'll take my chances with Bartell,' Dave replied evenly. Instead of replacing the star in his pocket, he pinned it to his shirt. 'Guess that makes it official,' he said tautly, 'and don't either of you forget it.'

He waited until Mawson had taken the keys from the wooden rack and escorted Cranton to the cells. Once he heard the metallic clang of the door closing and the key being turned in the lock, he spun on his heel and left. What Mawson would do now, he wasn't sure; possibly he might warn Bartell as soon as he could find him.

He reined up at the far and of the street and glanced back in time to see the sheriff's portly figure hurrying along the boardwalk in the direction of the Lost Trail saloon. Evidently, his suspicions had been correct.

What Bartell's intentions would be on hearing the news of Bender's death was more uncertain. Dave couldn't guess what the outlaw would do. The man was both cunning and devious. Whatever happened, Dave hoped that Bartell would still go ahead with his plan to hold up that train. If he was right, the only piece of the jigsaw which was missing was the knowledge of when this hold-up would take place.

Less than an hour later, having made sure that he was not being followed, he reached the shack in the hills. Thorpe was already there with Marie and Seth. There was a fire blazing in the wide hearth, sending a pleasant warmth through the room.

'What happened in town, Marshal?' Seth asked.

Standing in front of the fire, Dave said: 'It was just as I figured. Mawson wasn't goin' to lock Cranton in jail until I showed him my badge. As I was leavin' I spotted him making his way to the saloon, no doubt to inform Bartell of what's happened.'

'I figure you'd better watch your back from now on,' Thorpe said, his tone deadly serious.

'I intend to. The only thing I need now is information concernin' that gold-shipment. My guess is that once Bartell has finalized his plans, he'll ride out o' town with all his men. Until then, he'll lie low in Sioux Falls.'

'There ain't many in town who know me.' Thorpe spoke up from the other side of the room. 'I'm sure neither Bartell or any of his men have seen me before.'

Dave ran a hand down his cheek. 'It's possible he may remember you from the war.'

Thorpe shook his head. 'We were all at the front. He was stationed at our headquarters. Maybe he's heard my name but he's never seen me.'

'Then I'd like you to stick around town and keep an eye on him.'

'I can do that too,' Seth interrupted.

Dave shook his head. 'No, old-timer, that would be too risky. Cranton knows who slugged him and you can be sure he'll talk. I'm also too well known to Bartell.'

'And you reckon he'll still go after this gold, knowing you're here?' Marie asked, warming her hands at the fire. 'He may think you've been in touch with the Army and rather than risk everything, he'll take what he's got and head for the border.'

'That's a possibility,' Dave admitted. 'But I'm bankin' on him carryin' out this one last big hold-up. He's a gambler and an addict. Even if a couple of his men get killed, it'll mean nothin' to him just so long as he comes out alive. Take my word for it, I've been trailin' this *hombre* for so long I know him almost as well as he knows himself.'

Thorpe cut several slices of venison from the deer he had hung, thrust them on to a spit and placed them over the fire. Straightening up, he said softly: 'All right, Dave, I'll go along with your plan. I just hope it works – for all our sakes.'

'What do you aim to do now?' Wharton asked.

Checking his guns, Dave said calmly: 'Once I've had a bite to eat, I'm ridin' out to see a rancher friend o' mine. I think he ought to know that Jesse Bender ain't going to bother him again.'

Ned Bartell's face was a blend of mixed emotions as he stared across the saloon table at the sheriff. Mawson had just told him that Bender was dead, shot by this marshal who had ridden unannounced into town. Contrary to what Bender had believed, Bartell had had little use for him, considering him more of a liability than an asset.

Bender had been a fool in thinking he was a match for Stevens, and now he had paid the price. However, this presented Bartell with a problem. It was just possible that the men Bender had hired would seek their revenge on this marshal and if that happened there could be an all-out range war between them and the other ranchers. If that happened, it could bring some unwelcome attention to Sioux Falls from the authorities and that was the last thing he wanted.

The information he had received was that the

gold-shipment was due to be made in two days. He already knew the route that train would take and the particular spot he had chosen for his attack lay less than twenty miles from town, where the railroad ran through a long narrow cutting.

He was well aware that Woodrow and the others were getting impatient, especially with this marshal in town but he figured he could hold them together for this one, final raid.

'You got any idea where this goddamn marshal is now?' he growled. 'I figure it's time I got rid of him once and for all. He's been hounding me for long enough.'

Mawson took a long swallow of his drink. He was afraid of the man who faced him across the table. Now, without Jesse Bender to back him up, he had never felt more vulnerable in his life.

'After he forced me at gunpoint to lock up Cranton, he headed out o' town.'

'You know which way he went?'

'He headed north, I think.'

Bartell downed his drink and poured another. 'Hell, he could be anywhere. That's rough country out there and I can't afford to send any o' my men after him.' Leaning forward, he forced himself to analyse the situation clearly. Whatever happened, he didn't want any trouble in town for the next couple of days.

Sitting forward on the edge of his chair, Mawson waited for the other to go on. At last Bartell said gruffly: 'Here's what I want you to do. Let Cranton go, tell him to get all o' Bender's men together and scour the country to the north. There are only so many places where this lawman can hide.'

The sheriff finished his drink and rose to his feet. 'I'll do that right away.' Turning, he hurried out of the saloon, glad to be away.

Dave rode into the courtyard fronting Carlton's ranch house shortly after darkness had fallen. He had followed a circuitous route around the town, coming upon the spread from the south. There were lights burning in the windows and off to one side he noticed the burnt-out ruins of the stable.

The door opened as he swung down from the saddle. Carlton stepped outside with a rifle in his hands, moving quickly to one side so as not to be silhouetted against the light. The rancher must have recognized him at once for he lowered the Winchester and came forward with rapid strides.

Looking closely at Dave's face, he said tautly: 'Somethin' wrong, Dave? Guess you've heard about the fire.'

Dave nodded, looping the reins over the rail. 'I've heard. I came to tell you that you'll have no more trouble from Bender. He's dead.'

He saw the sudden gust of surprise that flashed across the other's features. 'Dead? How the hell did that happen?'

'He kidnapped Marie Devlin, took her up to the old mine-workings. I trailed him there and shot him.'

As he led Dave into the house, Carlton said; 'I guess that's the best news I've heard in a long time. You've done the town a favour gettin' rid of that critter. I've been talkin' to the other ranchers. They finally saw things my way. They've agreed to band together and—'

'Can you get them all together tonight, Ben?'

'Tonight? But—'

'Bender had one of his men with him up there in the hills, a fellow by the name o' Cranton. I brought him in and ordered Mawson to keep him in jail. Somehow, I figure Mawson's turned him loose. By now, he'll be ridin' back to that ranch with news that their boss is dead. If we hit 'em now, we can finish 'em for good.'

Carlton hesitated but only for a moment. 'Sure. You don't reckon they'll ride out now they've no one to work for?'

'Maybe. But this way we'll make certain.'

Carlton nodded. 'Give me half an hour to collect all o' the others,' he said. He threw Dave an oblique glance. 'Will you ride with us, Dave?'

Dave gave a grim smile. 'I reckon it's my duty to get rid o' men like these,' he said. 'How many men do you figure you can count on?'

Strapping on his gunbelt, the other replied: 'Forty, maybe more.'

'Good. I've no idea how many men Bender had on his payroll, but my guess is they won't be expectin' us. That'll give us the advantage o' surprise.'

Less than an hour later they were all gathered in a wide stand of trees. Lights were visible in the darkness a quarter of a mile away where Bender's place stood in a long valley. Several men could be seen in the courtyard but there was little sign of activity.

Clearly, the men were not on the point of moving out.

Sitting beside Carlton, Dave said softly: 'Looks as though they ain't expectin' any trouble, Ben.'

'Guess not, but—' Carlton broke off sharply.

The sound of a fast-approaching rider broke through the stillness surrounding them. A moment later Dave caught sight of the man, down below, evidently coming along the trail from town. The rider rode straight into the courtyard and slid from his mount on the run.

Dave gave a nod. 'That's Cranton. Just as I figured. Mawson has let him out o' jail, probably on Bartell's orders. He's come to tell the others I shot Bender.'

Carlton made to urge his mount down the slope but Dave leaned sideways and caught at the reins. 'Hold hard, Ben. Let's first see what they intend to do. If they fork their broncs and ride out, we'll hit 'em on the trail yonder. if they go inside the house we'll spread out and hit 'em from all sides.'

'Guess that makes sense,' muttered one of the other ranchers. He signalled to his men to wait.

Down below, the men were gathered in a loose bunch, still talking. Then they moved off into the house, closing the door behind them. Dave gave a brisk nod. 'Right. Half of you go that way and take 'em from the rear. We'll wait until you're in position and then go in at the front.'

'It's not goin' to be easy makin' a frontal attack,' Carlton said. 'Those walls look pretty stout to me and we could be cut down before we're halfway across that courtyard.'

'They won't be expectin' us,' Dave said thinly. 'Some of us can give coverin' fire from here with rifles.'

Waiting until half of the men had moved away through the trees to circle around the house, Dave kept his gaze fixed on the ranch. There was the occasional movement of a shadow across the windows but nothing else. Evidently those men in there were trying to decide their next move. He knew that a lot would depend upon any further orders Cranton got from the sheriff.

Then, sliding one by one from their saddles, the men moved forward through the fringe of trees. There was a stretch of rough ground between them and the edge of the courtyard, dotted with bushes and tufts of coarse grass.

Turning to Carlton, Dave murmured: 'Tell your men to get under any cover they can find and be ready to rush the house once I give the signal.'

Leaning sideways in the saddle, Carlton opened his mouth to speak but at that moment one of the men called out in a harsh whisper: 'It looks as though they're intendin' to ride out.'

Throwing a quick glance across the open ground, Dave saw that the door had opened and the men were emerging, moving towards their mounts. Before the first man could reach his horse, Dave squeezed the trigger of his Colt. The leading man staggered and spun round as the heavy slug took him in the chest. Throwing up his arms in a last despairing effort to keep life in his body, he pitched backward against the hitching rail. Wood splintered under him as he fell.

Taken completely by surprise, Bender's men stared wildly about them. The light from the windows showed them all in stark silhouette making them easy targets. Some succeeded in getting back inside the house but the others, caught in the open, struggled to find cover along the veranda, throwing themselves flat on the wooden boards.

Keeping his head well down, Dave aimed swiftly at the stabbing lances of gunflame from the men near the wall. Two of the men suddenly lurched to their knees, clawing at their chests as slugs burned their way into them.

Swiftly, the return fire from the men trapped outside diminished but there were still several holed up inside the building. The harsh staccato of shots from the rear of the ranch house told Dave that some of the gunslingers were attempting to escape in that direction and had run into the men he had sent round to the rear.

Swiftly, he pulled his head down as a bullet hummed past his cheek like an angry hornet.

It was soon obvious that the men inside the house had them effectively pinned down and were not going to give up without a fight.

Turning to Carlton, he hissed, 'Give me some coverin' fire.'

The other caught at his arm. 'You're not goin' to try to rush the place? God man, that would be sheer suicide. You'll never reach it.'

'Can you come up with a better idea?'

Carlton reluctantly released his grip. 'I reckon you

know what you're doin' but I still think you're a danged fool to try it.'

Getting his legs under him, Dave waited as a savage volley of rifle fire poured into the front of the building. Then, sucking in a deep breath, he threw himself forward, doubled up, sprinting for the cover of the long veranda. Bullets kicked up spurts of dust around his feet as he ran. Then, miraculously, he reached the veranda and threw himself down.

More shots whistled thinly over his head as he crouched down. There was a window almost directly above him. All of the glass had been knocked out of it by the defenders inside. Slowly, he worked his way to his right until he was out of sight of anyone inside, then quickly vaulted the low rail.

He waited for a moment until the firing from the trees stopped, then eased himself along the wall, pressing his shoulders hard against the wood as he approached the nearer of the two windows. He knew the men inside would be kneeling behind them, possibly wondering why the shooting had ceased. The sound of low voices reached him as he paused at the side of the window.

Grasping both Colts tightly, he waited for a second, then thrust himself forward, squeezing both triggers, aiming almost blindly. A dark figure rose up in front of him. He had a fragmentary glimpse of a bearded face as he pushed the barrel against the man's chest and fired. The other fell back with a muffled cry, crashing on to the floor.

Dave was only marginally aware that Carlton and the rest of the men were rushing forward. A moment later the front door fell in with a resounding crash. A volley of further shots sounded and then there came an unnatural silence. Carlton stared about him, lowering the smoking Colt in his hand.

'I guess this finishes it,' he said thinly. We won't have any more trouble from them.'

'Now there's only Bartell to take care of,' Dave replied. He turned sharply at a shout from one of the men.

'This one is still breathin' but I don't reckon he's got long to live.'

Dave went over and stared down at the man lying on the floor. 'It's Cranton,' he muttered harshly. He went down on one knee, and stared into the bearded face. 'So you were plannin' on ridin' out o' the territory now that Bender's dead.'

Cranton's face spasmed. He swallowed hard and tried to speak but for several moments no words came out. Running his tongue around his twisted mouth, he managed to say: 'We ain't quitters. We weren't runnin' out, Stevens. Bartell's orders were to find you and kill both you and the girl.'

A harsh rattle sounded deep in his throat and his head fell limply to one side.

CHAPTER IX

THE PRICE OF GREED

'You still believe there will be another shipment o' gold and Bartell knows all about it?' Seth asked. There was a note of doubt in his wheezing tone.

They were standing in the clearing in front of the shack. The sun had lifted from behind the trees half an hour earlier. Two days had passed since the attack on Bender's spread and there had still been no word from Thorpe, who was keeping watch in town for any move that Bartell might make.

'There'll be one and he knows every little detail about it,' Dave replied confidently. 'To my way o' figuring, he already knows the time and which route that train will take. I'm sure he's already made his plans.'

'If you're intendin' on followin' him, he'll have a head start on you. You'll never catch up with him before he hits that train.'

Dave gave a wry grin. 'That ain't any part o' my plan, Seth.' He glanced round quickly as Marie came to the door.

'Just what are you planning to do, Dave?' She had evidently overheard his last remark.

'Once he and the gang get their hands on that gold I'm bankin' on him sticking to his usual routine. He has to come back by the trail to the south o' town. He'll send his men on ahead to Sioux Falls while he takes the gold to wherever he's hidin' it. That's when I'll follow him.'

'Then I'm going with you.' There was a note of grim determination in her voice. 'The job I was assigned to carry out was to find this gold and see that it gets back to its rightful owners.'

'Don't be a fool, Marie.' Dave spoke more sharply than he had intended. 'Not only is Bartell a highly dangerous killer but in that red dress you'd be seen for miles.'

'Maybe so. But I have more suitable clothing in my dressing-room at the saloon and with Bender dead and Bartell out of town, there'll be no danger going back there.'

'I still say you have to stay here.'

Marie's eyes flashed as she faced him. 'You have no jurisdiction over me, Marshal. Only the Pinkerton Agency can stop me. I take my orders directly from them.'

Seeing the look in her eyes, Dave knew it would be useless to argue any further. How well she would handle a gun when the chips were down, he didn't know.

He made to say something more but at that moment, Seth gripped his arm. 'There's a rider comin'.' he said hoarsely.

Five minutes later, Thorpe pushed his mount through the trees. It was evident he had ridden hard and fast. He dropped from the saddle and said: 'Bartell just rode out o' town, Dave. He was drivin' an old army wagon and had all of his men with him, includin' Cleaver.'

'Which way was he headed?'

'They took the south trail and they were in a hurry.'

'That's all I need to know. This is the only chance we're goin' to get of finding that gold. You'd better get a bite to eat and rest your mount. They won't be back for another four or five hours. Then we'll leave. Marie here insists on comin' with us. We'll have to stop off in town to get her somethin' more suitable to wear.'

There was a worried frown on Thorpe's lean features as he said; 'Meanin' no disrespect, ma'am but I don't figure it would be right for you to be in on this. Things could get mighty dangerous and—'

'I know what you're thinking,' Marie retorted acidly, 'that this is no job for a woman. But since I work for the Pinkerton Agency, neither of you has any hold over me. I was given the task of finding this stolen gold and that's what I mean to do.'

Shrugging resignedly, Thorpe went inside.

An hour later the trio rode out of Sioux Falls and took the trail leading due south from the town. Marie was now dressed in a short jacket, skirt and boots, and was sitting easily in the saddle. She had also buckled on a gunbelt with twin Colts in the leather holsters.

Glancing at her from the corner of his eye, Dave had the feeling she was a woman who could handle herself and would be well able to use the guns she wore.

There were no doubts in his mind about Thorpe. The lieutenant had fought in several campaigns during the war and could keep a clear head when things got tough.

Inwardly, however, he felt a nagging worry about Marie riding with them. It meant he would have to keep an eye open for her safety as well as his own. That affair with Bender must have tested her to the limit, yet she had instinctively known exactly what to do when Bender had held that gun to her head.

It wanted barely half an hour to noon when they arrived at the spot where the narrow trail angled sharply towards the east. A short distance to their right, several high bluffs rose out of the otherwise open ground. They provided the only cover there was for several miles.

Pointing, he said: 'That's where we'll wait for 'em. We'll be out o' sight o' the trail yonder.'

They turned their mounts and rode swiftly towards the massive pillars of rock. All around them the ground shimmered like water in the heat haze. Dave could feel the sunlight beating down on his head and shoulders as he swung out of the saddle.

Glancing around, he noticed the small hollow which cut back into the rock, forming a space wide enough for them and the horses. Here they were out of the direct sunlight but in spite of this there was no respite from the oppressive heat and he knew it would get worse as the afternoon progressed.

'Now all we can do is wait,' Thorpe commented. He took out tobacco and paper, rolled a cigarette, and lit it, inhaling deeply. Marie drank a little of the water from her canteen, swilling it around her mouth before swallowing. It did little to slake her thirst.

Stepping a little way out of the hollow, Dave scanned the terrain towards the west, to where a line of hills stood out as a purple smudge on the horizon. For the first time he realized just how difficult it was going to be to trail Bartell. Out there, three riders could be seen for several miles, not only by the outlaw but by his men making their way back to town. It was also possible that this time Bartell would take his men with him, share out the gold, and head straight for the border to make good their escape.

Thorpe came forward and stood beside him, following the direction of Dave's gaze. 'You thinkin' the same thing as I am?' he asked quietly.

Dave gave a brief nod. 'It's goin' to be mighty tricky followin' Bartell without being seen if he heads in that direction.'

Pondering on that for a moment, Thorpe remarked: 'It's not likely Bartell would bury that gold in open ground around here. He'd have to put up a marker to be sure he could find it again and that would make it easy for any of his men to spot if they cane out here lookiin' for it. My guess is it's somewhere in those hills yonder.'

'That would seem the logical place,' Dave agreed. He threw a swift glance at the sun. He knew he had to make a decision – and quickly, while there was still time. After only a momentary pause, he said decisively: 'I reckon we should take a chance and head for those hills. If we ride fast we can reach 'em before that gang gets back. From there, we can watch this whole territory.'

Without asking any further questions, Thorpe tossed his cigarette butt on to the ground and motioned to Marie. 'There's been a change o' plan,' he explained. 'We've decided to ride for those hills yonder. This ground is too open for us to have any chance o' following Bartell without bein' spotted.'

Marie acquiesced instantly without any questions. They climbed back into their saddles and headed out, pushing their mounts to the limit. Riding a little way ahead of the others, Dave cursed himself for not having recognized this problem earlier. He had no idea how long it would be before those outlaws returned and it was now essential that they should reach the cover of the hills and their dust trail dissipate before Bartell could spot it.

He had the feeling that Marie was not used to this hard riding but, glancing occasionally over his shoulder, he saw that she was keeping up with them, her face set into lines of grim determination. As they reached the tree-covered slopes of the hills he threw an all-embracing glance behind him and let out a sigh of relief.

The terrain was still empty, clear to the distant

horizon. The long trail of dust they had left in their wake was dispersing rapidly. Turning back in the saddle, he motioned swiftly to his companions. 'Get in among the trees a little way. From here we can spot Bartell clear to the trail.'

Edging their mounts forward, they pushed into the stand of tall trees that bordered the arid land they had just crossed. Here there was little space between the broad trunks but somehow they managed to dismount, looping the reins over the low branches.

Slowly, the afternoon wore on. Still the open country to the east remained empty. The distant buttes which marked the position of the trail were clearly visible in the harsh sunlight, throwing stark black shadows across the ground beside them.

Even though Thorpe had said that Bartell had taken the army wagon with him, Dave was beginning to think they had made a mistake. Then Marie clutched his arm.

'There!' She pointed through the narrow gap between the trees.

Squinting against the glancing sunlight, he was just able to make out the small group of black dots in the far distance. 'It's them all right,' he muttered.

They watched tensely as the outlaws made their way along the trail, keeping together in a tight bunch.

'They seem to be in a hurry,' Thorpe remarked after a brief scrutiny. 'I just hope there ain't any soldiers on their tail. That could spoil everything.'

Dave switched his gaze slightly, watching the rear

of the oncoming men. He could see nothing to indicate that Bartell and his men were being followed.

'It could be that Bartell ain't too keen to be out in daylight with all that gold,' he suggested harshly.

They watched intently as the outlaws reached the bend in the trail. Here they halted and there seemed to be some kind of argument going on. Then the crash of a single gunshot reached them faintly from the distance and they saw one of the men reel in the saddle and drop to the ground beside his mount.

'What the hell. . . ?' Thorpe muttered.

Dave gave a grim smile. 'It seems that Bartell is havin' trouble keeping his men on a tight rein. Reckon they don't like the idea of him takin' that gold to his secret hidin' place. Probably they don't trust him to share it out.'

The stand-off lasted for several minutes. Then the remaining men wheeled their mounts and headed away, taking the trail towards Sioux Falls. The bulky figure of Ned Bartell remained seated in front of the wagon, watching them leave, ignoring the man sprawled on the ground.

'Once those others are out o' sight, I reckon he'll head this way to where the rest o' that gold is hidden,' Dave said confidently. He turned his glance on his companions. 'Remember, no shooting until I say so. My guess is he'll watch his back every inch o' the way in case those men have other ideas.'

In the distance, Bartell was now standing on the board of the wagon, whipping the horse to even greater efforts. It was clear to the watchers that the animal was tiring rapidly yet Bartell flogged it mercilessly. He repeatedly threw wary glances over his shoulder, still apparently unsure that the men he had sent into town were not trailing him.

At last he seemed to be satisfied that his orders had been carried out. He hauled slightly on the reins, turning the wagon towards a point a little to the left.

Following his course, Dave said softly: 'There must be a trail yonder that leads up into these hills. Somehow, I doubt if he'll figure on anyone bein' here. Once he gets on to that track, we move out and follow him.'

Ten minutes later they saw the wagon move into the dense fringe of trees less than 200 yards away. Cautiously, they eased their mounts out of cover. In the near distance it was possible to pick out the sound of the horse and wagon making its laborious progress upgrade.

They soon came upon the rough track almost completely hidden from view by thickly tangled branches and undergrowth. The stony path was narrow and they had to make their way in single file. With Dave in the lead and Marie bringing up the rear, they put their horses to the steep incline, making as little noise as possible.

The dull rumble of the wagon was still audible and Dave guessed that Bartell was some 200 yards ahead of them, still climbing the steep slope. Then, abruptly, the sound stopped. Instantly, Dave raised his right hand, bringing his companions to a halt. straining to pick out any sound, he waited tensely.

Either Bartell was suspicious and had brought the

wagon to a halt, or he had turned off the track into the trees. The silence lengthened as Dave debated his next move. Then, after taking out his Colt, he gigged the stallion slowly forward, his eyes alert for any ominous movement. Twenty yards further on, the track ran straight for fifty yards but there was no sign of the outlaw.

Then Thorpe uttered a low hiss. Dave turned and saw that he was pointing to their right. There, almost completely hidden by the underbrush, was a narrow path. On either side, the grass and low bushes had been flattened by the passage of heavy wheels.

Nodding, he pulled on the reins and led the way through a veritable jungle of twisted branches and Spanish thorn. The path angled across the side of the hill, eventually ending on the edge of a wide open area. He cautioned the others to remain where they were, slipped from the saddle and went forward to get a better view.

On the far perimeter of the clearing were several old adobe buildings, clearly abandoned many years before. He could see nothing of Bartell but the wagon stood in front of one of the houses. A moment later the outlaw emerged through an open doorway. He went to the wagon took down a large wooden box and carried it inside.

Dave motioned Thorpe and Marie forward. When Bartell reappeared, Dave stepped forward a couple of paces, his gun levelled on the outlaw. 'Hold it right there, Bartell,' he called loudly. 'Make one wrong move and it'll be your last.'

Bartell's head jerked up in stunned surprise. Then

his thick lips creased into a grin. 'So you finally caught up with me, Marshal. I must say it took you some time. Nearly four years, ain't it?'

'That's about right. But this is the end o' the line for you. I reckon you got just a little too greedy.'

Bartell shrugged. 'There's plenty here, Stevens. More than you'll ever see again. Even if we share it out with your partners, we'll all be set up for life in Mexico. Think about that before you do anythin' stupid.' He glanced quickly towards Thorpe standing a few feet away. 'I'm sure you wouldn't mind a share, mister.'

'No deal, Bartell.' Thorpe shook his head. 'Even if I was interested, I wouldn't trust you an inch. You're now willin' to sell out your partners in town. I guess that would happen to anyone else who went in with you.'

'So what do you intend doin' now – shoot me down in cold blood?'

'I'm takin' you back to Sioux Falls, and this time I'll make damned sure you stay in jail until the circuit judge arrives,' Dave said thinly. 'I reckon you know what the sentence will be and that goes for the rest o' your men. Now move slowly and unhitch that horse.'

Bartell hesitated and then moved towards the front of the wagon, bending towards the traces. The next instant, moving more quickly than Dave had anticipated, he had snatched up a Winchester, grabbing it in both hands.

Dave heard Marie's warning cry an instant before he brought the Colt to bear. He squeezed the trigger twice. Even with two slugs in his chest, Bartell somehow remained on his feet. There was a wolfish grin on his fleshy features. Then another shot rang out, the bullet hitting him between the eyes.

Bartell fell sideways against the wagon. The Winchester went off as he fell, the bullet going high into the trees. Slowly, Marie lowered her gun.

From a short distance away Thorpe said admiringly: 'That was mighty fine shootin'. Guess I was wrong about bringing you with us.'

Dave went inside the low building, ducking his head. There were several of the boxes placed against one wall, together with a shovel. A careful examination of the earthen floor revealed where other holes had been dug and cleverly filled in.

He went back outside. 'It looks as though this is where he hid all that gold,' he said. 'Reckon we should—'

He broke off sharply as Thorpe spoke. 'This is where I take over, Marshal. I'm takin' this gold. Reckon I could be across the Mexican border within an hour and I know a little place where even Bartell's men will never find me. Now drop your gunbelts, both o' you.' A note of menace had entered his voice.

'So this is what you had in mind all the time,' Marie said bitterly. 'All that talk about avenging those men who died because of Bartell's treachery meant nothing.'

Thorpe's lips curled into a faint smile. 'Sure I felt sorry for 'em, but they're all dead now and this gold is for the livin'. Now toss your guns into the middle o' the clearing where I can see 'em.'

Slowly, Dave unbuckled his gunbelt and tossed it on to the dirt as Marie did likewise. Inwardly, he cursed himself for not recognizing that the sight of all this gold could turn men into killers.

Keeping his weapon trained on them, Thorpe said harshly: 'Now you're goin' to dig up those boxes and load 'em on to the wagon.'

'And then you mean to kill us and leave us here where no one will find us,' Marie said.

'I guess that's the way of it. I sure wouldn't like the two of you on my tail when I head for the border.'

He moved towards the open doorway and motioned Dave inside. To Marie, he said: 'You stay beside the wagon where I can see you.'

A moment later he stepped back a couple of paces as Dave came out, carrying one of the boxes with both hands. In that second, Dave realized they had only one chance. Glancing up, he saw from the look on Marie's face that she had also recognized it.

As he stepped forward, he released one hand on the rope handle. The box tilted downwards, one edge hitting the dirt. Swiftly, Dave bent to pick it up, knowing that Thorpe's attention was momentarily on him.

'Watch what the hell you're doin' with that box,' Thorpe rasped angrily. 'If you—'

Before he could finish his sentence, the single shot rang out, echoing across the clearing. Thorpe twisted, an expression of disbelief on his face as he stared down at the blood on his shirt. The Colt slipped from his nerveless fingers as he fell forward on to his face in the dirt.

Marie came forward, holding the Winchester she had snatched from Bartell's dead hand. 'I think this is the end for him too,' she said simply. There was no trace of emotion in her tone. 'We'd better get back to town and I'll send word for the Agency to come and pick up the gold.'

Dave nodded. 'I guess it'll be safe here until they come.'

Marie gestured towards the two bodies lying on the ground. 'They won't be able to tell anyone where it is and somehow I think I can trust you to keep this to yourself.' There was a faint smile on her face which Dave hadn't seen before.

'Then the only ones we have to worry about now are Bartell's men. They're still in town and once they hear that Bartell is dead, they'll either ride clear out o' the territory or try to find the gold for themselves. Either way, it's my job to stop them.'

After carefully burying the rest of the boxes, they made their way back to Sioux Falls, with Dave driving the wagon with the two bodies in the back. The sun had set by the time they drove into the main street. With twilight falling, the saloons were just beginning their nightly trade.

Dave reined up outside the sheriff's office. He stepped down, then stopped as he saw Mawson coming out of the Lost Trail saloon. The sheriff paused uncertainly as he caught sight of them, then turned and went hastily back inside.

Dave reached up and caught Marie's hand. 'Get down!' he hissed urgently. 'Get under cover across the street.'

Marie slid from the saddle and asked tautly: 'What is it?'

'Mawson's just seen us. My guess is that Bartell's men are in the saloon yonder and he's gone to warn 'em.'

Together, they ran across to the opposite boardwalk and crouched behind a long water-trough. Less than a minute later the batwing doors of the saloon swung open and four men came out. Dave recognized Cleaver and Mawson and knew his surmise had been right. He felt sure that, even in the deepening twilight, the sheriff had recognized Bartell's huge bulk lying in the wagon and had passed word along to the others.

The four men spread out slowly in front of the saloon, peering in all directions, unsure of where he and Marie were.

Keeping his head down, Dave called loudly: 'Drop your guns – all o' you. Bartell's dead and that gold is goin' back to where it belongs.'

'Damn your hide, Marshal, you ain't taking any of us in for trial.'

Dave didn't recognize the voice, but a moment later gunfire erupted across the street as the men threw themselves down flat on the boardwalk. Slugs hammered against the trough, sending splinters of wood flying over their heads.

On either side the street, which had been crowded with townsfolk, had suddenly emptied. Aiming swiftly, Dave fired at a shadowy shape crawling towards the doors of the saloon. He saw the man sway and go down on to his side. Clearly, he had been hit, but somehow he pushed himself to his knees, one hand reaching for the door.

In that moment Dave recognised Mawson. From a couple of feet away, Marie fired in a single fluid movement. The sheriff threw up an arm in a last despairing effort before his back arched and he fell into the street with one leg tangled in the hitching rail.

The remaining three continued to send a withering fusillade of shots across the street, knowing they were pinned down and possibly hoping that one of their shots might find its mark. Then Dave heard the hammers of his Colts click on empty chambers.

Almost as if it had been a signal, all three outlaws lurched to their feet and came running forward, weaving from side to side. Desperately, Dave struggled to force fresh shells from his belt into the Colts.

One of the men suddenly stopped in midstride, his legs buckling beneath him as Marie fired twice. Cleaver, his face twisted into a scowl, managed to get halfway across the street before Marie dropped him with her last bullet. The third man reached the boardwalk a minute later.

Grinning viciously, he levelled his Colt on Dave. 'This is where you and your interferin' lady-friend get it, Marshal!' he gritted harshly. 'Guess I'm the only one left alive to collect all that gold. Now you get it first and then the woman.'

Dave knew there was no chance of getting off a single shot before the other pulled the trigger. Staring up, he saw the gun barrel lowering until it pointed directly at his chest, the man's finger hard on the trigger.

The next second a shot shattered the silence in the street. Instinctively, Dave threw himself to one side. Stunned, he saw the outlaw's body jerk and twist violently from the waist as the heavy slug took him in the side.

For a moment Dave couldn't tell where the rifle shot had come from. Then, at the edge of his vision, he noticed the figure twenty yards along the street holding a Winchester.

Wharton came over. 'I guess I can still aim straight with this old gun o' mine,' he said soberly. 'I saw you ride into town with Bartell's body and guessed his men might be out to get you once they learned he was dead.' He paused, then added: 'What happened to Thorpe?'

As he helped Marie to her feet, Dave said thinly: 'I guess greed got the better of him. He tried to kill us and take it all for himself.'

'He must have had it in mind all the time,' Marie said. 'Once he learned of the plan to follow Bartell he made sure he went with us. We got Bartell first and then he saw his chance. With us out of the way he could take the wagon and be over the border into Mexico within a few hours.'

Dusting down her skirt, she added: 'I'll get word through to the Agency about the gold.'

When she had gone Seth dug inside his jacket pocket and brought out a folded piece of paper which he handed to Dave. 'This message came for you a couple of hours ago. I figured it might be important.'

Dave walked across to the saloon and read the

message in the shaft of light coming through the wide window. Then he put it into his pocket. 'It's from Coulson, from Major Cauldwell. Seems we were right when we figured Bartell had to have two spies inside the Army headquarters. Cleaver was one and the other was Lieutenant Delmore.'

Wharton glanced round at the four bodies lying in the street. 'I guess your job here is finished, Marshal. You'll be headin' back East, I reckon. Now the town's rid o' Bender and those outlaws and Mawson's dead, the town committee will be lookin' for a new sheriff.'

Dave noticed the glance which the old-timer threw in his direction and shook his head vehemently. 'I ain't takin' on the job' o' sheriff,' he said fervently. 'Matter o' fact, I'm thinkin' I've seen enough o' gunplay and killin' to last me a lifetime.'

Wharton's expression turned to one of surprise. 'You're quittin' as a federal marshal?'

'That's it, I guess.'

'Then what in tarnation do you intend doin'?'

'I think it's time I settled down. Carlton offered me a job on his spread. This is goin' to be a good town once they elect a sheriff who can keep law and order. Someday there'll be a branch of the railroad here and—'

'Somehow I think that might not be a bad idea.' Marie had returned and was standing close beside him. 'I guess you know there's a reward for the return of that gold. With that money a man could buy a ranch of his own.'

'The trouble is,' Seth butted in, 'it ain't easy for a man to do that alone.' He threw an oblique glance in

Marie's direction as he spoke.

'That had occurred to me too.' There was a warm glow at the back of her eyes as she smiled and slipped her hand into Dave's. 'That's why I quit too. They weren't too happy about my decision but they understood when I told them my reason for it.'